DEBTS

FRANKIE ROBERTSON

Castle Rock Publishing
Tucson, Arizona

DEBTS

"A great tale of adventure and romance, beautifully imagined and deeply engaging from beginning to end!" ~**Diana Gabaldon,** bestselling author of *Outlander*

"Grabs you from the start with excellent pacing, fascinating characters and culture, and a satisfying romance. I want more!" ~**Jennifer Roberson,** bestselling author of the Sword Dancer series, The Chronicles of the Cheysuli, and *Lady of the Glen*

"Romance, peril, and magic: what more could anyone ask?" ~**Dennis L. McKiernan,** author of the Mithgar series, and the Faery series

DEBTS

Copyright © 2014 Frances R. Gross

Cover art and formatting by Jaycee DeLorenzo
of Sweet 'N Spicy Designs

Published by Castle Rock Publishing.

http://www.CastleRockPublishing.com

*For Caroline and all the others who said,
"Where's the next one?"*

acknowledgments

Although writing is a solitary occupation, a book usually comes into being influenced by a number of people. Among those who aided and supported me along the way:

Jennifer Roberson, Kathleen Kirkwood, Caroline Mickelson, and Tara Simone have been, and continue to be, an endless source of information and inspiration.

Earl W. Parrish, Roxy Rogers, and Jill Knowles for taking time out of their busy lives to put eyes on this manuscript and make suggestions for improvement.

The Tucson Romance Writers of America chapter for giving me opportunities to learn and grow as an author.

Jaycee DeLorenzo, my cover and interior designer, for making this book look better than I could have done by myself.

Thank you all.

PROLOGUE

On A Midsummer's Eve

ANNIKKE'S SMILE HELD a bitter edge as Benoia sneaked a peek into the huge iron cauldron hanging in the yard. Annikke knew the girl half expected to find human bones in the bottom, and she thought about letting Benoia's imagination stew for a while. Maybe she should cook dinner in the big old pot tonight and let Benoia guess at the menu. But cleaning the cauldron was a major undertaking and cooking for two in it would be absurd. Besides, if she spooked the girl too much she'd be next to useless.

Annikke sighed. Time to put a stop to this.

"It's just a big old pot, girl."

Benoia jumped like she'd been caught pilfering. Her bony hands clutched each other near her throat, causing the thin cloth of her ragged sleeves to fall back, revealing meatless forearms. The girl would need a week or three of decent meals before she could do any useful work.

Annikke looked down the narrow lane that twisted into the spring wood, but Benoia's father was no longer in sight. Annikke spat anyway. He'd traded his daughter's indenture for a posset to fight a fever in his wastrel son. The boy would recover his health now, but she rather thought that she and Benoia had got the better of the deal.

If I had a daughter, I wouldn't sell her so cheap.

But what chance was there of that? A woman needed a man to get a child, and no man would look twice at Annikke, let alone bed her.

"Come along, girl. The coop needs cleaning."

The oil lamp flickered and Annikke looked up from her sewing to catch Benoia staring at her from under lowered lashes. Nearly a month of hearty food and light work had put a bit of rose in Benoia's cheeks, but no smile in her eyes. Annikke never raised a hand to the girl, but she remained timid and fearful.

"What are you looking at?" Annikke asked sharply.

Local gossip made much of the fact that Annikke had been Fey-marked some ten years ago. She'd gone missing her twelfth year at midsummer, when she was a girl in bud as Benoia now was. A month later, when her parents found her asleep in the forest, her hair had turned silver. Not grey, nor white. Silver.

Annikke had no memory of that missing time. Her parents had said nothing about it, but for the rest of their lives they'd not looked at her the same—when they could bear to look at her at all. Even so, Annikke might have found a way to pretend nothing had changed, except that her hair wouldn't let her. She'd tried covering her head with scarves and hats, but the younger children had taunted her and dared each other to snatch them away. No dye would take. She'd even tried shaving her head once, hoping that her mousey brown hair would grow back in place of the gleaming silver, but to no avail. Now she wore it long and defiantly, falling like a river of moonlight down her back. She'd taken to wearing dark gowns, too, to show it off.

Benoia flinched and dropped her eyes to the mending in her small hands. "Nothing, ma'am."

Frigga's fat fanny. Nothing.

She'd fed the girl and given her good clothing to wear. Was a small scrap of gratitude, a flicker of warmth, too much to hope for in return?

Of course it is.

Why should she expect Benoia to be any different from the other village folk? They came to her quick enough for her healing potions, but not one of them would offer her a smile of friendship. She was Feymarked. How could she have let herself think otherwise?

"Do you want to go home?"

Benoia looked up at her. Was that hope in her wide blue eyes? It made Annikke want to spit. The stupid little chit would rather return to a father who beat and starved her than do easy service with her.

Annikke knew the stories that fed Benoia's fears. *The Elves and their minions still visit her when the moon sails high, and lie with her in the forest glades.* So the farm wives whispered. *It's the Elves,* they said, *who teach her about the herbs she uses to heal, and tutor her in their Fey Magic.* Annikke shook her head. If she knew Elven Magic, she'd hardly need to take in an ungrateful child to help with the chores.

"Good. Home you shall go." Annikke paused, then wiped the girl's shocked expression away with her next words. "In a year's time, just as your father pledged."

Midsummer night promised a new moon and a dark night for the Elves to walk abroad and dance in the starlight. Annikke shivered despite the summer's warmth. She'd make sure that she and Benoia were buttoned up tight inside the house before full dark.

Annikke leaned against the porch railing, watching Benoia as the sun slipped below the tops of the trees. Insects buzzed and the swallows skimmed low over the meadow as Benoia pulled clothes off the line and carefully folded them before putting them in the basket. She always did her tasks well. She never tarried or slopped her way through. After three months the girl still feared her too much to relax.

"Hurry up. It will be dark soon."

Benoia jumped and nodded.

The girl had been especially skittish today. She probably thought Annikke would offer her as a sacrifice to the Elves tonight if she didn't do her chores right. Annikke turned to stir the pot where the stew simmered, considering. Was Benoia stupid enough to run off? Or was she more afraid to be abroad on Midsummer's night than she was of Annikke? She hoped so. Even if the girl was a foolish little thing, Annikke didn't want Benoia coming to harm.

Movement in the shadows of the forest lane caught Annikke's eye. Fear slithered down her spine and her breath stuck in her throat, yet she managed to force an urgent command past her lips.

"Benoia, to me."

The girl looked up sharply, and then scurried to obey.

A well-favored man emerged from the wood, coming into view around the bend in the trail. His shirt sleeves were rolled up and the tunic laces across his chest were loose, but the cloth and leather were of fine workmanship. A sword with a silver pommel hung at his side and he led a lame horse.

Annikke waited silently, heart speeding, one hand clutching a large wooden spoon like a weapon.

"Greetings, mistress. Is there a farrier in the village yonder?"

The young man stopped close enough to talk, yet far enough away to not offer threat.

Courteous. Or maybe it was her silver hair that caused him to keep his distance. But his eyes held no guarded wariness.

"Aye," she answered, "but you'll not get there before dark and he'll not welcome a stranger tonight."

"Has he so much business, then?"

Annikke smiled grimly despite a little rill of fear. "Who are you that you're so unconcerned to be out on Midsummer's night?"

"My apologies, mistress. I am Lord Fendrikanin Kendersson, sworn to Lord Dahleven of Quartzholm."

A Lord, then, and some distance from home—or so he says. She dared not turn him away though that was precisely what she wanted to do. "You might as well share our supper and spend the night here."

She wouldn't normally ask him into the house. Not with her and a young girl alone. She'd heard about some of those young lords—if lord he truly was. He had not appeared until the sun was behind the hills. He could be an Elf venturing out early this night, disguised by Fey glamour.

"Thank you mistress." Lord Fendrikanin grinned despite her ungracious invitation. "Where shall I make my bed?" His eyes were teasing and boyish, for all that he was a handsome, broad-shouldered man. Or seemed to be.

Annikke clenched her jaw. He was laughing at her.

She answered him through gritted teeth. "In the house, of course... my lord. Benoia will give up her cot to you."

But before she let him cross her threshold, she would know what it was she hosted. She gestured to the huge iron cauldron with her wooden spoon. "We'll sit to dinner in a moment, my lord. But will you first help me pour out this wash water?" If he were Fey, he wouldn't touch the iron pot. *Couldn't* touch it without it burning him.

Lord Fendrikanin showed no affront at being asked to help with the chores. He tied his big bay to the porch railing and strode without hesitation to the large pot where it hung on its tripod. "Where do you want the water, mistress? Yonder in your garden?" He nodded his head toward the lush herb patch as he lifted the heavy cauldron by himself.

His muscles bunched under the weight of water and iron, but he showed no sign of pain.

Annikke released a breath she hadn't realized she'd been holding. *Not an Elf Lord, then.*

"No. No, thank you, my lord. The herbs are too fragile for such a rush of water. The edge of the yard will do, if you please."

As Lord Fendrikanin emptied the water and replaced the cauldron on its hook she glanced at his mount where it stood favoring its right front leg.

Ashamed of the cold welcome she'd given, Annikke said, "I am somewhat skilled with herbs and healing, my lord. Would you have me look at your horse?"

"I'd be grateful." Lord Fendrikanin smiled at her, sending unexpected warmth dancing through her.

Annikke nodded, trying to hide her reaction. "Benoia, come closer. It's time you learned something of herb-craft."

It was nearly full dark by the time Benoia completed applying the poultice to the animal's leg. Lord Fender, as he asked to be called, held a lamp to see by.

"Well done, girl. Well done." Annikke rubbed the nervous sweat from her hands. It was long past time to be inside.

Benoia looked at Annikke with a shy smile and pride glowing in her eyes.

Annikke felt a prick of shame. *Is that the first time I've praised her?*

After dinner, Annikke and Lord Fender continued to talk long after Benoia had fallen asleep in her cot. He had refused to take the girl's bed from her, saying it was too short for him, nor would he accept Annikke's. He'd declined her offer very prettily, too, and without suggesting she share it with him.

But she was Fey-marked after all. No sane man would want to share her bed.

It was late, long past time to retire, but Annikke couldn't sleep. She never slept on Midsummer's night. Lord Fender showed no sign of fatigue either, but continued chatting away. Somehow he teased the story of her silver hair from her. Most of it. She didn't want to speak of the last part. Maybe this year it would stop.

"I'm surprised you didn't seek out the Daughters of Freya when the local folk shunned you," he said when she'd finished her tale.

His words shocked her. She'd seen no disgust or revulsion in his eyes, but now he said this?

"You think me fit only for the company of whores and witches?"

Lord Fender shook his head. "No, mistress. Gossip

has wronged the Daughters of Freya just as it has you. I should think you would be less believing of such ugly rumors. For the most part they are women without the protection of family who have come together to support one another. I think they would welcome you."

Annikke stared. He was a lord, yet he spoke well of the Daughters of Freya? There was a tale there. "How is it that you know—?"

A single sharp knock at the door cut off her question.

Annikke gripped the arms of her chair tightly. It was happening again. They'd come back—as they did every Midsummer's night.

Lord Fender looked at her questioningly. He must have seen the dread in her face because his posture grew alert. "What is it?"

Fear gripped her throat. She could only shake her head mutely.

"Someone must be in desperate need to seek a healer on this of all nights," he said. "Shall I see who it is?"

Another knock came. Two raps this time.

Lord Fender rose from his chair.

"No!" She flung out her arm to stop him.

Every Midsummer's night for the last ten years the knocking had come, rapping persistently for entrance. Till the end of their lives, her parents had kept the house closed shut those nights, even in the warmest weather. For all they couldn't look at her, they wouldn't let their only child be stolen from them a second time.

Three raps.

Had she hoped that having Benoia here, and Lord Fender, would somehow keep them away?

"I'll not let any harm come to you or the girl, mistress." Lord Fender went to the door, his hand on the hilt of his long dagger. "Who seeks the healer?" he called through the closed door.

Four loud reports.

"Speak or depart!" Lord Fender shouted, drawing his blade.

Benoia stirred on her cot, and the fire popped, but otherwise all was still. No further knocks sounded at the door.

Could they be gone so soon? Usually the rapping lasted for a candlemark or more, but then, she'd never spoken to them. Her parents had forbidden it those first years, and later, when she was alone, she'd been too afraid.

Lord Fender looked at her in question, but all she could do was shake her head while clenching her sweaty palms in her skirt. He had just turned to resume his seat when the door reverberated with five sharp blows.

Suddenly Annikke could stand it no longer. She wanted it to stop. It *had* to stop. Now. Tonight. How dared these folk bring fear into her life year after year? She jumped up from her chair and threw open the door. "Be gone! Trouble me no further! Have you not tormented me enough?"

Lord Fender jerked her back from the door, interposing his body between her and the visitors. Abruptly he stopped, drew a sharp breath, and sagged against the doorframe, his dagger held loosely at his side. Annikke peered past his shoulder.

"I am Gaelon," her visitor said. "I've come to repay my debt."

On her porch stood an Elf. Two others waited in the yard, one with his hand pointed almost casually toward Lord Fender. The near one stood tall and slender and strong like a loose limbed colt. His feathery brows arched delicately, and his bright green eyes slanted over high cheek bones. Hair bright as sunlight on water fell past his shoulders. He was beautiful—and Fey.

A splash of shock stole Annikke's breath. She recognized him.

"What—what do you want here?"

"We have sought these last twelve summers to settle our debt to you. Our honor, and our Elders, require us to make amends for the wrong we did. Your life here among your own people is not what it would have been. We will make a place for you among us."

"No!" Benoia screeched. She jumped from her cot and rushed forward, throwing her arms around Annikke's waist.

Startled, Annikke put an arm around Benoia. "It's all right, girl," she murmured, though she had no faith that it was.

The young Elf raised an eyebrow in surprise and smiled. "She's a pretty one you've taken in, and her Talent is a rare one. Not many are immune to our glamour. Mayhap she'd like to join us, too."

Horror cascaded down Annikke's spine as his true purpose became clear. It was Benoia he really wanted. Another young girl to bedazzle and destroy. Annikke glanced up at Lord Fender. His face was relaxed and he stared out the door as if he no longer saw what was before him. He'd be no help. Him, they had under their glamour.

"You will not take this child." Annikke held Benoia tighter and spoke as if she really had a hope of defying them.

Gaelon looked disappointed. "Very well. But what of you?"

"You're the one who stole me! Why? Why did you destroy my life?"

Gaelon actually looked away. She hadn't thought an Elf would feel shame. Then his clear green eyes found hers again. "You helped me win a wager fifteen summers gone. I—"

"A wager? A wager! What *wager* was worth my life?"

"My companions said no human's Talent could make an *alarion* seedling grow as fast as one of us could. *I* said you could." He said it proudly, as though he had championed her.

Annikke stared at him, dumbstruck. For that, for *that,* he'd stolen her life away?

She'd always loved that her Talent, the bit of magic that each person developed at puberty, had taken the form of making things grow. Now it seemed sullied. It was her Talent that had condemned her.

Gaelon hurried on before she could vent her outrage. "Your Talent is strong, and I won the wager. I owe you for that, and for the changes I brought to your life. Life among the *Lios Alfar* is pleasant. You enjoyed it before. Will you return with me?"

Changes? He utterly destroyed her life and he called it *changes*? "Why would I want to return to what I have no memory of?"

"That I can remedy," he said, reaching out.

She jerked back, but not before he touched the side of her face.

She remembered.

Trees that cuddled her like a beloved child. The sweet, sharp taste of fruit that quenched thirst like a mountain stream. Water that laughed and sang with a friend's voice. Music that made her heart break with its loveliness, and laughter that danced through the soul. And the Elves. Beautiful, remote, tall, and elegant.

She sighed. "So beautiful."

"Please, mistress, don't go!" Benoia's plea came from where her face was buried in Annikke's shoulder, startling in its vehemence. Had she so misread the girl's feelings?

"You could rejoin your family early, Benoia," Annikke offered, hating the idea of returning her to her brutish father.

"No! I want to stay here. Teach me herb-craft. Teach me to heal. Please!"

"If you stay with me, some will say you are Fey-marked as well. Have you thought of that?" She asked gently.

Benoia had enough sense not to answer right away. She paused for a moment, and then gazed steadily up into Annikke's eyes. "Let them talk."

Annikke's heart threatened to choke her. Benoia would risk so much to stay with her?

"Come back with us, Annikke," the Elf said. "You were happy among us. We'll take good care of you."

It was true. She'd been well cared for among the Elves.

What did she have to keep her here, except Benoia?

Annikke looked down at the girl's pleading eyes, felt Benoia's strong warm arms clasped tightly around her waist. She had Benoia. Benoia, who *wanted* to stay with her.

"No. I don't belong there."

Gaelon's face fell. "But I must make amends."

"You have nothing I want."

"Mistress," Benoia said softly. "Don't be so quick." She turned to the Elf and swallowed nervously before asking, "Could you give my mistress a husband?"

Annikke choked. *What?* How could the girl have guessed how lonely she was?

Gaelon laughed. "Of course! Will this man do?" He gestured at Lord Fender.

"No! You mustn't!" Annikke exclaimed.

"He's very handsome, mistress," Benoia urged. "He'd give you beautiful babies. And I don't think he'd beat you, even without the glamour upon him."

Gaelon raised his hand. "Speak and it shall be so, Annikke."

"No! You can't give me another's life in exchange for mine."

Gaelon's hand fell to his side again. "Then what?"

Annikke shook her head. What could she ask for? He must give her something, or he'd be back next summer, and the next after that, rapping on her door all Midsummer's night until he repaid his debt. What could compensate her for what he'd stolen?

She stood silent for a long time, thinking of what she'd lost, and what she longed for. Gaelon and Benoia held their peace, waiting as the stars glittered overhead.

"I am already known to be Fey-marked," she finally said. "I might as well have something besides my hair to show for it. I am skilled in herb-craft, but there are many whom I still cannot help. Give me some of your knowledge of healing."

Gaelon laughed. "Of course! And a touch of the magic that goes with it too!"

"I want only what I can pass on to Benoia," she said looking at the girl. "If you want to learn."

Benoia's smile made her face shine like the sun on a summer's day. "That would be a welcome gift, indeed."

The sun rose clear and bright, burning away the mist that lingered at the edge of the forest. The poultice had reduced the swelling in the foreleg of Lord Fender's mount, but it still favored the leg.

"I'll have to lead him all the way back to Quartzholm," Lord Fender lamented after walking the bay around the yard. Though he spoke calmly enough, he still seemed unsettled by the night's events, and anxious to be on his way.

Annikke cast a cautious glance at Lord Fender. "Perhaps not."

Kneeling beside the horse she drew several runes in the dirt around its hoof. She cupped her hands around his leg and murmured, *"Falle til ro, hest. Dyrkke, hele. Falle til ro og hele."* Her fingers tingled and her palms grew warm as she invoked Gaelon's gift. When she'd done, the horse stood on the leg showing no sign of pain and rubbed her with his velvet muzzle.

Annikke laughed. "I'll take that as a thank you."

Lord Fender gave her a sober look. "I thank you as well, mistress. But you should be careful whom you let witness that."

Annikke returned a level gaze. "I'll be careful, as will Benoia. And we'll not speak of you or those other—visitors," she assured him. "I may be Fey-marked, my lord, but I'm not addled."

Lord Fender gave her a small smile. "That you clearly are not. You made a good bargain, mistress. You'll be happier with this gift than you would have been with me."

"Freyr and Freya!" Annikke felt the heat rise in her face. "You heard that?"

"The Elves must have let their glamour slip enough so I could know how my fate was decided." Fender lifted her chin with gentle fingers. "You are fair, Lady, and the man who takes you to wife will be fortunate indeed, but I thank you for letting me choose my own path. I am in your debt. If ever you are in need, call upon me."

Annikke nodded. "You are most welcome, my lord. And if ever you travel this way again, you have a place by my fire, just—please—don't come a-knocking on Midsummer's night!"

chapter one

Five years later

"i'm off." benoia hefted a basket stocked with oint-ments, tisanes, and powders as she announced her departure.

Annikke glanced up from the dried herbs she was grinding. "Be back before twilight."

Her foster daughter chuckled at Annikke's stand-ard warning, but nodded. "I only have three visits to make. I'll return long before then."

It had been five years since the Elves had settled their debt with Annikke and promised to leave her and Benoia in peace. They'd kept their word and stayed away, but Annikke suspected they still watched her cot-tage and never felt easy being out and about past sundown.

"I could go with you," Annikke offered, even though it was foolish of her to think of it. At seventeen summers, Benoia was a woman grown. She was well able to make these visits, and there was work enough to be done here at the cottage. The weeds in the herb patch required her attention and Benoia's circuit included a stop at Granny Mallow's, who was so set in her ways she still made the ward sign whenever she saw Annikke's silver hair.

Benoia's lips thinned and she tossed her long brown braid behind her back. "I'm delivering potions near the village, not going all the way to Quartzholm. And even if I were, you've taught me well. I can do whatever you could."

"Aye, you could. But don't." The girl was skilled in the use of the healing magic the Elves had given them, perhaps even better than Annikke, but Benoia was young and full of spirit. She itched to use her Fey gifts, even though the villagers would shun her for it if they understood what she was doing. "Just—be mindful of an old woman's fears and be careful. Please?"

"Old woman? Pah! You're no more an old woman than I am." Benoia dropped a quick kiss on the top of Annikke's head. "You worry too much," she said as she slipped out the door left open to the early summer breeze.

Annikke stared after the girl, a little envious of her carefree youth. She was barely ten summers older than her foster-daughter, but she felt older. Benoia's soul was still light, carrying no shadow from her father's indifference and neglect. "Perhaps I do worry too much," she murmured, "but I have reason." She lifted the mortar again and continued grinding the dried fevercool leaves into dust.

Annikke had just finished sealing several pots of ointment with wax when thunder rumbled overhead. She looked up, realizing that the small main room of the cottage had grown as dim as twilight, though it was only mid-afternoon. Then she saw Benoia's cloak hanging from its peg by the door. Summer storms in the mountains could be icy and violent. The air already held a shiver. The girl would be drenched without her wrap.

Benoia has sense enough to wait out the storm.

Nevertheless, a creeping unease crawled up the back of Annikke's neck.

She promised to be home before twilight. She could be caught in the downpour trying to hurry home.

But it wasn't fear of Benoia taking a chill that drove Annikke to snatch their cloaks and hurry out. Just off the porch, she paused. The sky was grey and heavy with unshed rain and shadows writhed beneath trees tossed by the wind. The path that led through the forest, where the Elves had stolen Annikke years before, was dark with the storm-wrought gloaming. She'd neither seen nor heard from them since they'd paid their debt to her, but even now she felt their eyes upon her—though it was probably only her imagination.

"Damn them. Let them look." Annikke tightened the drawstring of her hood, and hurried to find Benoia.

The girl would have gone to Farne's home first to check on his wife. Elin had borne the blacksmith a fine strapping son two weeks back. It had been a hard delivery, but both mother and son were strong and doing well. The visit was more to reassure the blacksmith than anything else. Farne was maybe two summers older than Annikke, and he'd never teased her about being Fey-marked when they were children. For that alone Annikke would check on his wife until the lad was grown and married if that would ease the blacksmith's mind.

From there, Benoia would have gone on to Granny

Mallow's farm as it was the farthest away, before stopping at the cottage of Lord Tholvar's dairyman. The man had come out the worse from an encounter with a bull. It had taken all of Annikke and Benoia's herb craft and Fey gifted magic to save him, but he was on the mend now and only needed his bandages checked and a potion for his pain.

The track to the dairyman's croft split off to Annikke's left, and though the path was dark and overgrown from little use, Annikke gritted her teeth and strode forward as if she felt not a whit of fear. If the Elves were watching, she wouldn't let them think her cowed.

The roar of the wind lashing through the branches overhead nearly covered the scream. Fear jolted like lightning through Annikke's breast, stealing her breath.

Benoia!

Without a thought, Annikke hiked up her skirts and ran.

Closer now, Benoia's angry screams were clearer.

"No! Get off me! "

A cry of pain cut through the wind.

Annikke barely slowed as the path curved hard to the left and then back to the right circling an ancient oak and her children. The screams grew louder, filled with agony and terror. Annikke rounded the thicket. Fifty feet beyond, a man lay on top of Benoia, with her skirts shoved up to her waist.

Rage crashed through Annikke, more violent than the coming storm. She charged forward, heedless that she had nothing but her empty hands to protect Benoia with. She was almost upon them when she realized it was the man who was screaming.

Annikke didn't stop. With strength she didn't know she had, she jerked the man away from Benoia and flung him to one side. He didn't resist, just curled into a ball as his screams subsided to moans. When Annikke saw he wouldn't renew his attack, she turned her attention to her foster-daughter, quickly searching the girl's body for wounds, but finding only scrapes and the beginning of bruises. With a tender touch she brushed hair from Benoia's purpling cheek.

"Oh, my sweetling. You're all right now," Annikke murmured. She prayed to Freya she spoke the truth. Benoia's heart might be more wounded than her body. She'd been timid and beaten down that first day she'd come to live with Annikke. Would this attack drag her back into her childhood fear?

The worry had barely formed before Benoia sat up, and then stood, pushing Annikke's hands away. Benoia held her fists rigidly at her sides as she glared at the young man still rocking on the ground, clutching his privates.

"My balls!" He groaned.

Benoia must have kneed him. *Good for her.*

"Nothing a cold soak and a few days of rest won't cure," Annikke said. "You're getting away with less than the beating you deserve." She put an arm around Benoia and realized the girl was shaking—just as she did after using her healing magic. She needed warmth and hot food. It was only then that Annikke noted she'd dropped Benoia's wrap back by the oak. She wrapped her own body-warmed cloak around the girl's shoulders and turned her toward the path home.

"What did you do to me?" Anger, fear, and pain mingled in the man's voice. He rolled up to sit, then struggled to push himself another few feet away from them, using only one leg.

A tremor ran through Benoia's slender frame and Annikke tensed, ready to defend them against a renewed attack, even as the shock of recognition speared her heart with fear. This was Sveyn, Lord Tholvar's heir.

He had a reputation for taking what he wanted, but whether he was at fault or not, his father would not let his son be harmed without raining retribution down upon them.

Heedless of the staring women, the young lord pulled down the open flap of his trews, revealing a shrunken cock so dark with bruising it was nearly black.

Sveyn screamed and clutched at it. "Oh gods! Oh gods!"

"Oh my dear girl, what have you done?" Annikke murmured.

"He was hurting me."

"Yes, my dear. You had to protect yourself. But what did you *do*?"

"I stopped him." Benoia's voice was cold.

"You crippled me!"

Despite the tension and purpose in her posture, Benoia's simple answers revealed how shaken she was. Annikke needed to get her foster-daughter away from here. She left Sveyn rocking back and forth in the leaf mold, and guided Benoia back through the forest to their home.

chapter two

ANNIKKE SWEPT UP and donned Benoia's cloak as
they passed the oak, then kept her arm around the girl
all the way back to their two room cottage. The trees
continued to lash their boughs overhead in the wind,
their leaves complaining noisily. She wouldn't be able to
hear if someone pursued them, and a follower would be
hard to spot among the shifting patterns of dark and
darker.

The track was narrow, not really wide enough for
two abreast. Low branches and bushes tried to clutch at
their cloaks but Annikke invoked her Talent for influ-
encing plants, waving them back until they passed. The
single magical Talent that all developed in youth came
as effortlessly as sight or hearing. Hers was best suited
for making plants grow strong and healthy, but it could
also discourage weeds from taking up residence in her
garden. Pushing these bushes back didn't harm them.
They merely pulled back to give them room to go by. In
fact, as she and Benoia progressed, the undergrowth be-

gan to anticipate them, withdrawing before Annikke needed them to, then relaxing after they'd gone by. Annikke noted the oddness, but gave it little thought. Her concern was all for getting Benoia home.

Benoia continued to shiver as she did when she'd used the healing magic, but whatever her foster-daughter had done, it wasn't healing. Now was not the time to question her, however. Her pace slowed them, but at last they stepped onto their porch and into the cottage. Stillness fell around them like a warm blanket when Annikke shut the door behind them. She gently pushed her daughter into the rocking chair, and set about making tea. The routine of building up the fire and filling the kettle soothed her nerves. Gradually, the stark reality of what they must do asserted itself despite the calming routine of pouring steaming water over the herbs.

As soon as Benoia steadied, they had to leave. Given the way Sveyn had been moving, she thought his leg might be withered like his cock. That would slow his return home, but despite that, it wouldn't be long before Lord Tholvar sent men for her and Benoia. He was the ultimate authority in this province. No one would intercede for them, and Lord Tholvar wouldn't care that his son had been about to rape Benoia. If past history was any indication, he would think the girl ungrateful for the honor of his son's interest.

The storm broke at last, drumming the roof with furious rain, echoing Annikke's anger.

The healing skills she and Benoia had been given had gradually overcome most of the villagers' fearfulness of her Fey-marking. The two of them had hidden the source of their skill, and the villagers hadn't asked questions, not when their loved ones survived injuries and illnesses that would have felled them without Annikke and Benoia's care.

Now that hard won acceptance had to be cast aside, thanks to that selfish, spoiled, lordling.

Benoia stilled her rocking when Annikke pressed a mug of honeyed tea into her hands. "Drink, my dear. You'll feel better."

Her foster-daughter sipped, then drank half the mug. Annikke sat at the table, sipping her own tea, watching the younger woman as color returned to her cheeks. Her shivering stopped, and eventually the girl raised her gaze to meet Annikke's, but she quickly looked down again at the amber liquid in her cup.

"I'm sorry. I've ruined everything."

Annikke's heart clenched, hearing the girl's bleak tone. "No. It was Sveyn. The fault lies with *him*, and only him."

"But I ... I *hurt* him."

Annikke recalled the sight of Sveyn's shriveled cock. "It was no more than he deserved," She said fiercely.

"But if I hadn't—"

"Look at me." She waited until Benoia raised her gaze to meet hers. "Do not suggest that you should have let that—that Loki-spawn take you by force. Do not even think it."

"But I used magic against him. I didn't know I could do that! It just happened when he ... when he tried to..."

Annikke hadn't known that their magic could work in reverse, causing harm instead of healing, either. The Elves hadn't told them. She and Benoia had used the gift intuitively, helping where they could. They'd explained away the effects of their magic as herb craft for the last five years, and the villagers had accepted that because it had helped them and their loved ones. Now it would be seen otherwise. Even those they'd healed would fear them, assuming they lived long enough to be feared.

"We have to leave here," Annikke said.

"But where will we go? Once Lord Tholvar names us Outcasts, every man's hand will turn against us."

Annikke remembered a debt still owed her. She hoped the young lord who'd made it would keep his word. "To Lord Fendrikanin, in Quartzholm."

chapter three

AREN BIRGIRSON STOOD to one side of the practice yard, waiting for Lord Fendrikanin to finish his lesson with the Jarl's wife, Lady Celia. He'd been summoned here because it had been he who had found the man stealing the silver from the lower halls and selling it to traveling merchants in the village. He'd hoped his success where others had failed would bring him to Lord Fendrikanin's notice. All he had to do now was convince the young lord to take him into the Jarl's service. Simple, once he actually had the man's attention.

"Celia, you're still dropping your guard!" Lord Fendrikanin threw up his hands in disgust.

"You try guarding this much territory!" the woman shot back, indicating her gravid belly with the foot long blade of her wooden practice dagger.

"You're leaving openings for attack as big as a whale, woman," her trainer rejoined while repositioning her stance.

"I'm not your woman."

"Thank Baldur for that!" Lord Fendrikanin smiled, taking the sting from his words. Aren watched as the man assumed a stance opposite her again. Without warning he attacked her, shouting, "Bitch! Whore!"

The ugly words and abrupt action jolted Aren into taking a step forward to protect her, but just as quickly he recognized the training tactic for what it was, an effort to shake the Lady's focus. She didn't waver in her defense, however. As pregnant as she was, she took a quick gliding step back, holding her knife at the ready and presenting her right side to her foe. "To me! To me!" she shouted as her maneuver forced her attacker to take another step to maintain his advance. She continued retreating as Lord Fendrikanin pursued her around the training yard.

Other men standing around the perimeter watched and commented to each other, but none bellowed the encouragement or insults they would have shouted to one of their fellows.

"Enough." Lord Fendrikanin held up his hands. "Well done, Celia. You have mastered the most effective knife fighting technique I can teach you."

"Run away and shout for help." The lady panted with effort but still managed a wry grin. "Between my lack of skill and my girth I suppose that *is* my best strategy."

"If you don't like my training philosophy, Lord Dahleven would be more than happy if you'd stick to practicing the bow."

"After six years of lessons, and being well into my third pregnancy, I probably ought to agree, but enemies tend not to stay at sufficient range to be archery targets, Fender. As you know all too well."

What enemies would a Jarl's wife encounter in the nursery?

Aren had been in Quartzholm long enough to hear

songs of Lady Celia's exploits, but he'd assumed they were exaggerations as all such tales were. If Lady Celia was training to defend her babies, perhaps the city was more dangerous than he'd thought. Had he erred in bringing his mother and daughter here? From what he'd seen, Quartzholm was an orderly place under Lord Dahleven's rule. No longer the seat of the Kon—that was now Dalrik, the home of Lord Magnus—Quartzholm was frequented by Light Elves and Tewakwe. Even so, the city was prosperous.

Lord Fendrikanin tossed a towel to the lady, wiping his face with another. "Then I'd recommend you let a guard run point for you, my lady, for carrying a babe or not, the knife is not your weapon."

Lady Celia stuck her tongue out at her trainer. "It would be a fairer fight if you had a twenty pound sack of grain strapped to your waist."

The lord merely laughed. "Your enemies won't do so."

The Lady shrugged acknowledgment of his point.

"You did well today, but I don't want to see you on the training field again until at least two months after you're safely delivered."

The tales were accurate on this at least; Lady Celia was not a conventional lady.

"As much as I'd like to, I can't disagree." Lady Celia tossed Lord Fendrikanin her towel and stretched, her hands in the small of her back. "I'm getting tired faster than I did with the first two."

"You didn't have a little lord and lady to keep up with then," Lord Fender said.

"True enough." Celia laughed. "I'm off. First a bath, then a nap," she said as she left them.

Lord Fendrikanin drank a ladleful from the water bucket as the other men resumed their training. When he'd slaked his thirst he joined Aren in the corner of the practice yard. "You're Aren Birgirsson, the man who Tracked the fools filching the silver."

"Yes, my lord. Though they were not fools, or they would not have evaded the men you first sent after them."

"Indeed? And how is it that you found them when the others failed?"

Suddenly Aren saw the danger he was in. Did this lord suspect him of being complicit in the thefts and of turning on his fellow thieves? "My Talent for Tracking is not quite the same as others'. Where most use Talented observation, I feel where my quarry has gone. I *know* their path. I cannot explain it better than that."

The young lord nodded. "And what reward would you ask?"

"I want to serve Lord Dahleven, my lord."

"You left your home to serve the Jarl?"

"Yes, my lord."

"And you brought your mother and daughter, as well."

"You are well informed, my lord." Aren cringed inwardly. *How much else does he know?*

The corner of the other man's mouth curled up as if he'd heard Aren's concern. "It's my honor to serve Lord Dahleven. I take that duty very seriously."

Aren bowed his head. He understood what Lord Fendrikanin had left unsaid. "Then you know my father was an Oathbreaker," he said quietly.

"I do." Lord Fendrikanin's tone was grave. "I know he swore loyalty to Lord Fellig, and then failed to answer a summons when called to arms. I do not know why."

Aren lifted his head to meet the other man's measuring gaze. "What does it matter? He failed in his duty. I will not. My mother and I have lived on the far edge of respectability since my father's shame. My daughter was born into it. I have provided as well as I could for them by hunting and selling furs. I'm good at what I do, and they want for nothing, nothing but the honor my sire stole from us.

"My mother is ill and my daughter is on the cusp of womanhood. They need their family honor restored. I ask only that you give me the opportunity to prove myself a better man than my father. Allow me to serve the Jarl."

The young lord was silent, while Aren held himself still, waiting.

"You reach high."

Aren's heart stuttered. He'd aimed high because he needed to overcome much. Had he wasted his chance?

"Will you serve me," Lord Fendrikanin continued, "and through me, the Jarl?"

Aren released a breath he hadn't known he was holding. "I will."

"Then I will accept your oath." Lord Fendrikanin drew his sword and presented the hilt to Aren.

Aren gripped the pommel and met the lord's gaze steadily and said, "I am Aren, grandson of Lars, known as Swiftfoot. I have come from Tracking cunning thieves and I will do yet greater deeds if you will accept my oath of fealty. I will fight for you, and not flee one foot from the battle. And when no battle causes the war horn to blow, yet will I remember my lord's generosity and offer service where I may. May Baldur witness my oath, and if I fail, may every man's hand turn against me and this sword pierce my disloyal heart."

The scuffle and grunts of effort had ceased around them. Lord Fendrikanin nodded, and spoke into the now silent yard. "I accept your oath. In return you shall be accorded all respect due one in my service. I will protect your family, provide weapons, shelter, sustenance and opportunity for you to prove your worth and earn glory for your family name. May Freyr and Freya witness my words, and Baldur hold me faithful and hallow this vow."

Relief leapt within Aren's breast. He knew he could prove himself, given a chance. His daughter would be able to marry well.

Lord Fendrikanin sheathed his sword. "With one caveat."

Aren held his breath. What condition would the lord put on his boon?

"In all dealings except the most formal, you will henceforth call me Lord Fender."

Aren grinned. "Aye, my lord. Lord Fender it is."

chapter four

with a task put before her, Benoia seemed to grow stronger. She gathered a change of clothes for each of them into a carry sack while Annikke packed food and filled the waterskins. She also filled a sack with products of her stillroom: rare herbs folded in cloth and several jars of ointments. Perhaps, wherever they ended up, they would again be able to use their skills, or at least they could sell their wares in the marketplace to gain a stake for a new beginning.

By the time they were ready, with packs, blankets, and oilskins, the rain had paused, but twilight had come in truth. Annikke hesitated just outside her door, looking at the herb garden she'd nurtured for many years, listening to the soft dripping of moisture from the eaves. The forest and its shadows loomed like a forbidding wall at the edge of the yard. The Elves had taken her from there, changing her life forever. She hadn't ventured into the forest at night since she was twelve summers old.

Memories of bright colors, Fey laughter, and song

teased, but Annikke pushed them away. She couldn't think of that. Not now. The Elves were cold, as was their beauty. And even though the villagers had shown her little warmth, desiring something so *other* was wrong. It only led to heartache. Humans and Elves were not meant to mingle. Her parents and the villagers had taught her that. And so for years she'd shunned the places the Elves traveled, including the forest.

The forest where they must now venture.

"We could wait until sunrise," Benoia suggested.

Annikke shook her head. "Tholvar won't wait. We mustn't either." She made herself step off the porch. "What may await us in the woods is less a danger than what will find us if we remain here." Annikke wished she felt as confident as her words implied. She took a step toward the trees, and then another, while her heart pounded.

Benoia followed.

At the edge of the forest Annikke paused again, her heart speeding. When she'd been a girl, she'd played in the shoulders of these woods, sometimes dipping into the green shrouded depths much further than her parents would have wished. She'd never felt afraid then, and she'd never gotten lost. The trees had felt like benevolent aunties, watching over her and never chiding her for forgotten chores. Now with darkness falling and the sky threatening further rain, all she could imagine were threats lurking in every shadow. Benoia touched her arm, looking up into her eyes with concern.

Annikke swallowed the tight knot in her throat. Her fear didn't matter. She couldn't let her foster-daughter be taken. She sucked a breath deep into her lungs and blew it out, then stepped into the trackless woods.

Shadow enveloped them as they slipped beneath the canopy. Pine needles and leaf mold quieted their steps. All that could be heard were insects and birds calling out their goodnight songs to each other. It wasn't long before the light was nearly gone and they had to stop. There was little undergrowth to hide them among the pines, but there were a few stands of oak. Annikke chose a spot on the far side of a thicket for them to bed down. Annikke spoke softly to the nurseling trees, stroking their slender trunks. By morning the little ones would have shifted, obscuring their path. If they were pursued, she hoped it would be enough to conceal them.

They spread an oilcloth on the ground before sitting to eat a bite of bread and cheese. Neither of them had much appetite, and soon they wrapped themselves in their blankets and the second oilskin. Annikke drew Benoia close, needing the feel of her daughter's warmth. The girl held her just as tightly, and soon Annikke felt tremors racking Benoia's delicate frame as the girl wept.

She'd been so brave. Benoia had defended herself, and she'd understood immediately that they needed to flee. She hadn't complained once about leaving all they knew behind.

"I'm so proud of you," Annikke murmured. "I thank the gods every day that they brought you to me. I could not ask for a better daughter."

Benoia's breath caught on a quiet sob. "But I've cost you everything."

"Hush. You've cost me nothing. All that's important to me is here in my arms."

Benoia's arms tightened around Annikke as she wept anew.

All Annikke could do was rub slow circles on her daughter's back until the girl fell into an exhausted slumber, her head pillowed on Annikke's shoulder.

Near dawn it rained again. This rainfall was gentle, as if the earlier storm had exhausted the clouds. They pulled the oilcloth over their heads and it kept them mostly dry. Annikke was glad she'd used pine wax to waterproof the canvas, its clean odor was much more pleasant in close quarters than the alternatives, and the smell blended with that of the trees.

The drizzle had tapered off when Annikke heard voices coming from the direction of her cottage. Men's voices, too far away for her to make out the words, but their tone was disgruntled. A kernel of satisfaction flowered in her breast. The men had probably thought to catch them easily, taking them by surprise in their beds.

Should she and Benoia try to slip away, to put more distance between them and their pursuers? Or should they stay still like rabbits, hoping to avoid unwanted attention?

A man shouted to another, nearer this time. "... forest?"

Beside her, Benoia startled awake and she put one finger against the girl's lips. Her foster-daughter nodded with the barest movement of her head.

Annikke wished she'd pulled some deadfall around them, or done something else to hide themselves better, but it had been nearly dark when they stopped. It was too late, now. All they could do was stay still.

Moisture dripped from leaves, pattering softly around them. Dim light filtered in under the edges of the oilcloth. Annikke's heart thudded and she held her breath, straining her ears, but the moist ground muffled the men's footsteps. Annikke couldn't tell if they were coming closer or moving away until a man stopped not twenty feet away.

chapter five

ANNIKKE STOPPED BREATHING, fearing the slightest movement would draw attention.

Too close, a man said, "This is a waste of time. Everyone knows she was afraid of the forest. She'd never come in here."

"We've looked enough to satisfy Tholvar's orders. Let's go," another man agreed from a little further away.

Footsteps that quickly grew too distant for Annikke to hear suggested they had left, but she and Benoia remained still for many minutes before carefully peeking out to look around. A thick mist hung in the air, turning trees into forbidding shadows. The man was right. She would never before have come into the woods, especially not on a day when Elven magic could hide behind every tree. Today, however, she gave thanks for the cloaking mist that had hidden her and Benoia.

Annikke paused, listening. She heard nothing other than birds chirping sleepily, and a squirrel scrabbling up the nearest pine.

Annikke breathed a sigh of relief. If the small creatures were out and about, the men must truly be gone. It wouldn't do to linger, though. They gathered their few possessions and departed, not pausing to break their fast.

Aren walked through the tunnels below Quartzholm with the Jarl's young nephew, Ari, by his side. Aren would have completed his assignment to locate Lord Dahleven's six year old grandniece, Kaleth, more quickly if he were on his own, but the boy was a treasure of information, so Aren welcomed his company. At eleven summers, Ari's Talent had not yet Emerged, but he was known to little Kaleth as Aren was not, and the boy's presence would set the little girl at ease when they found her.

Aren held his torch high as they came to a branching of tunnels and examined the dusty floor. Many feet had traveled these passages created hundreds of years ago by the Great Talents to facilitate trade and warfare. He could make out the occasional small print overlaying the others, but mostly he relied on his Talent which told him that Kaleth had gone down the right hand path.

"I never get lost down here, not the way some do," Ari volunteered. "I fell in the lake when I was five summers old and almost drowned, but I wasn't lost."

Aren's Talent told him they were close to finding the girl, but a jolt of alarm spiked through him at the mention of drowning. "Is the lake near here?"

"No. It's way over there." Ari waved his hand to the left. "It's really cold, not very good for swimming."

Aren blew out a breath of relief. "I'd guess not. Did the Jarl save you?"

"Uncle Dahben? No. He wasn't the Jarl then, anyway. The skalds say Aunt Celia breathed the 'breath of the gods' into me, but she says it's called rescue breathing. She's taught a lot of people how to do it, including me. I've also learned how to swim, so I won't drown again."

It was strange to hear the Jarl referred to by a family nickname. "I'm sure that's a relief to your father."

"Da is dead. He drank poison meant for the old Kon."

Aren felt a twinge of sympathy for the boy growing up without his father, but at least his da had saved the Kon and died a hero. And the boy wasn't without strong men to guide him.

"I promised Kaleth and Sorn that I'd teach them how to swim, but Uncle Ragni said we needed to have an adult with us." This last was said with a hint of disgust.

"You mean Father Ragnar, the Overprest?" The Jarl's brother and the head of the priests of Baldur.

Ari shot him a look perfected by the young when they knew something an elder didn't. "Yes, but we don't call him that."

"Who is Sorn?"

"Sorn is Uncle Dahben's heir. Sorn was Kaleth's Da and Uncle Dahben's sworn brother, and that's why he named his son after him. He died before she was born." Aren sorted through Ari's explanation and decided it was the Jarl's sworn brother who had died before his daughter Kaleth was born, and that Lord Dahleven had named his son after him. Aren could well imagine that neither the Overprest nor the Jarl would be willing to put the safety of the Jarl's firstborn in the hands of a child.

"Who taught you to swim?"

"Lord Fender. He knows where all the best swimming holes are. That's his Talent: Finding Water. He said he'd come with me when I teach Kaleth and Sorn."

"That's probably for the best."

"But I'm a good swimmer! And I'll be a man soon. I'm going to go through Emergence soon, I can tell. My Talent will be a really good one, too."

The two of them came to a four way split in the tunnels but Aren turned down the left-most without hesitation. A flicker of light soon confirmed his confidence that the little girl was close. "Kaleth?" he called.

"Kaleth!" Ari called immediately after. "Come here! Your mother's worried."

Aren signaled the boy to be quiet. Ari made a face, but he obeyed.

"Ari?" a little girl's voice answered.

Aren held their torch higher and picked up his pace. Around the next bend a six year old girl was standing at another meeting of the ways. Her torch was nearly burned out, sputtering as it sagged in her drooping arms.

"I got lost," she said simply. She didn't seem particularly upset by the experience.

Aren smiled. Kaleth had the same dark hair that his own daughter had. "And now you're found. Shall we take you back to your mother?"

"Yes. I'm hungry."

The little girl handed him her torch, which Aren passed on to Ari.

"You caused a lot of trouble, Kaleth. Everybody's looking for you. But we found you first! This is Aren. He's a Tracker."

Aren let the boy talk because he didn't seem to be upsetting the child. She was probably used to his chatter. He dug a piece of sugared fruit out of his pouch and offered it to the girl. "Here. This should hold you until we get you back above ground." Aren noticed Ari's eyes had fastened on the sweet, so he dug out another piece for the boy as well, and then led them back by the most direct route.

Aren carried Kaleth up a long stair to the courtyard. By the time they arrived, the little girl had fallen asleep on his shoulder. It had been nearly ten summers since he'd carried his own daughter, Tandra, that way, and it was with a twinge of nostalgia that Aren handed the slack-boned child off to her relieved mother. "She's well," he assured Lady Aenid. "Just tired."

From the sun's angle, Aren guessed that he'd been underground for not quite two candlemarks. Time enough to report to Lord Fender in the training yard, and then make his way home for the evening meal. As Aren turned to go there, he heard his name shouted. Lord Fender was at the top of the stairs leading into the castle, gesturing for Aren to join him.

At the top, Lord Fender clasped his hand in greeting. "Well done! Lady Aenid barely had time to work herself into a panic over her daughter. Lord Dahleven wants to thank you personally."

"The Jarl?"

Lord Fender grinned. "Kaleth is the daughter of his fallen oath brother and his niece. She's doubly dear to him."

"I was honored to serve."

Lord Fender clapped him on the shoulder. "And Lord Dahleven is honored to recognize your service. Come along."

Three flights of stairs and several long hallways later, Aren and Lord Fender were shown into an informal chamber by a guard with the swooping hawk emblem stitched on his left breast. Inside, a man of about Aren's age sat in one of two cushioned chairs drawn close to a cold fireplace. He wore a green suede tunic similar to the guards', but the swooping hawk embroidered on his chest was in gold thread. As Aren entered, the man set aside a sheaf of reports he'd been studying and rose. His russet beard was trimmed short in the style favored by younger men, but he braided his shoulder length hair back from his face so the gold hawk dangling from his left ear could be seen. He didn't need the finery he wore to communicate his rank, however. The Jarl wore his authority with ease, and no one in his presence would doubt his status.

"Dahl, this is Aren, the man I told you about."

Aren stood tall to meet Lord Dahleven. It was one thing to be one man among many in the Jarl's service. It was quite another for the Jarl to know you specifically, especially when your father was an Oathbreaker.

Lord Dahleven must have seen something in his eyes, because the first words he spoke were, "Yes, I know of your father's shame. But I also know you've done much to redeem your honor today. You have my thanks, and the thanks of my family." Lord Dahleven slipped a gold cuff from his left arm. "Accept this symbol of my gratitude for the service you have rendered us." He clasped the band onto Aren's forearm.

This was more than Aren had hoped for when he'd brought his family to Quartzholm. "I am honored to serve you, my lord."

"I'm glad to hear it, because I have another task for you."

chapter six

ΛΝΝΙΚΚΕ WΛS GLΛD that the oak thickets grew fewer as they moved deeper into the forest. The pines kept the undergrowth that clutched at their skirts to a minimum. Little grew in the soil blanketed with needles, just a few ferns and the rare orchid. Their travel would have been as easy as a walk in a lord's manicured garden if the layers of pine needles didn't hide rocky, uneven ground beneath. Their path looked smooth, but it took awareness and care to keep from turning their ankles.

"What will we do if Lord Fender won't help us?" Benoia asked when they'd stopped for a mid-afternoon rest.

"He will." Annikke dug into her carry-sack and pulled out an oatcake for each of them.

"But what if he doesn't?"

"And be an Oathbreaker? No. He didn't strike me as that kind of man."

"Who would know? It will be only our word against his and you're Fey-marked."

"Lord Fender would know. I was Fey-marked when he gave his promise. He'll keep his word."

"But what can he do? He wasn't there. He didn't see what happened. And if Lord Tholvar names us Outcast, who will believe us?" Benoia's tight grasp threatened to crumble her oatcake.

"Lord Fender will." Annikke put her hand over Benoia's. She understood the girl's fears. How alone and vulnerable she felt. "Don't borrow trouble. We aren't Outcasts yet." At least not as far as they knew.

"He could be cross-sworn," Benoia persisted. "An oath to Lord Dahleven would take precedence over a promise to a Fey-marked woman."

"Benoia." Annikke waited until her foster-daughter met her gaze. "Do not fret. Not all men are as faithless as your father. Lord Fender will keep his promise, and if he cannot give us aid, he will not hinder us. We'll go to the Daughters of Freya. They understand that women must sometimes take action when men forget their duty to honor and protect as Sveyn did."

Or so Lord Fender had told her. Annikke hoped it was true.

"Why don't we go there first?"

"I would not have you live your life with a cloud of accusation hanging dark over your head. Lord Fender serves the Jarl. He'll make sure you get a fair hearing."

Benoia fell silent and nibbled the edge of her oatcake. After a bit she said, "You should have sent me off on my own," she said in a small voice.

"I do *not* want to hear you say that ever again!" Did the girl really think Annikke could have lived happily, having cast off her foster-daughter like a broken dish? "You are my daughter, if not my blood."

Benoia's eyes filled with tears. She dropped her oatcake into her lap and covered her face with both hands as she began to sob.

Annikke gathered her into a tight hug. She rubbed the girl's back, letting her cry out the fear and anger of the attack, the grief of losing the only safe home she'd known, and the uncertainty of their future. Annikke's eyes filled as she grieved for the young woman in her arms.

Little more than five years ago Annikke's life had been barren of affection. Then Benoia's father had sold his daughter's indenture to Annikke, and Benoia had brought warmth into Annikke's carefully guarded heart. When Benoia's service had ended at the end of the year, her father had come for her, but Annikke had bought the girl's service for another year to keep her away from her father's belt. So it had gone, year after year. In law, Benoia was her thrall, but the law didn't govern her heart. As far as Annikke was concerned, the Norns had woven Benoia into her life as her daughter. She would not abandon the girl at the first test.

Lord Dahleven's steady grey eyes met Aren's. "Lord Tholvar came to me not a candlemark past, nigh frothing with anger, demanding that I send my best Tracker after the woman who injured his son. I would have you locate her and bring her back to Quartzholm for justice."

Aren bowed. "I'll leave at once, my lord."

Dahleven chuckled softly. "Your eagerness is to your credit, but tarry long enough to get the particulars. The woman in question is seventeen summers in age. Her name is Benoia and she is indentured to a Fey-marked woman."

"Annikke?" Lord Fender's tone held surprise.

Lord Dahleven's brows rose. "You know her?"

"I met her five years ago. She did me a service

when it would have served her not to, and she healed my horse of lameness. I believe the girl had only just entered service with her."

"Well, apparently this Annikke has aided Benoia's escape from Lord Tholvar's justice. I want to speak to her, also."

Lord Fender snorted. "His vengeance, you mean. What does he say happened?"

"He says Annikke taught her protégé Fey magic, and that the girl used it to cripple the young man's leg."

Fender groaned. "What provoked her to that?"

"Do the Fey-marked need a reason for the harm they cause?" Lord Dahleven's tone held a bitter edge.

Aren cringed inwardly and wondered what Lord Dahleven would think if he knew that Aren owed his life to a Fey. Even though the Light Elves had aided Quartzholm, most people still feared the Fey and regarded those touched by them as tainted. It would take more than a few songs of praise before folk changed beliefs handed down for generations.

"Aren, I would have you ask around her village about this woman," Lord Fender said. "When I knew her, Annikke didn't strike me as the kind who would condone harm being done to another. Not without cause." Aren's commander tipped his head and gave the Jarl a chagrinned smile. "If you are in agreement, my lord."

Lord Dahleven chuckled, apparently not offended by Lord Fender's presumption. "Indeed. Ask a few questions. But don't delay your search. Lord Tholvar may be a pompous, self-important ass, but I need his vote in the Althing to change the laws of inheritance. I finally have enough lords in agreement to allow direct inheritance by women, and I don't want to have to explain to Celia that it didn't pass because of one disgruntled and petty lord."

Aren suppressed a smile. Even so powerful a man

as a Jarl stepped lightly around his wife. Aren would too, if that wife were pregnant and had been learning to wield a knife.

"Your lady would not want the law passed at the cost of injustice, though," Lord Fender said.

Lord Dahleven shook his head. "No. Never that. So be thorough, Aren, but be quick."

chapter seven

it was too late in the day for Aren to leave for the village where Annikke and Benoia had lived, so he returned home to sleep in his own bed that night. The cottage he'd rented was sound, and not far outside the walls of the castle. Being close allowed his daughter, Tandra, to serve in Quartzholm's kitchen garden during the day and be home at night, and the Healers in Quartzholm were able to ease his mother's painful joints where those back home had not been. He'd worried about his decision, but uprooting his family from their familiar place on the periphery of their old village had been the right thing to do.

As usual, his mother fell asleep beside the fire after the evening meal, but at fifteen summers, Tandra was excited to hear every detail of his meeting with the Jarl.

"What's he like?" she asked, as she washed their wooden supper bowls.

Aren leaned back and slung one leg over the corner of the table. "He is a true leader of men, worthy of respect, and he wears his authority lightly."

"But is he handsome?"

He considered his daughter, who had come into her Talent of nurturing plants two years ago, and was now filling out her woman's body. Sometimes he noticed the young men watching her as she did her chores, and it filled him with trepidation. It wouldn't be long before she thought to marry. He needed to distinguish himself in Lord Dahleven's service so she could choose a husband worthy of her. "That depends."

"On what?"

"Do you think grey eyes and hair the color of burnt copper pleasing?"

"Ooh, yes! And is he tall?"

"I don't know. Am I tall?"

"You know you are. How does he compare?" Tandra stacked the last of the dishes on the shelf.

"He is perhaps a hand taller than I."

"And his shoulders, are they broad?"

"Broad enough to shoulder the responsibilities of the Jarldom—and the two children Lady Celia has already born him." Aren lifted a brow at his daughter, reminding her that the object of her interest was both married and far above her.

"Then he is indeed handsome. But old."

"He's not much older than I am," Aren protested, dropping his foot back to the unpolished floor.

Tandra laughed and he joined her, mingling is own deeper chuckle with her lighter toned mirth.

Aren departed when the eastern sky began to grey. Lord Fender had arranged for provisions and a swift mount, for which Aren was grateful. His old horse was at the end of its useful days, and was good for little more than carrying packages home on market day.

Lord Fender's directions to the village were clear, and Aren's mount got him there by noon with energy to spare. As he rode closer, Aren passed several narrow tracks that disappeared into the forest, but he stayed on the main thoroughfare, a dirt path barely wide enough for a cart. On the outskirts of the village he was greeted by a woman hanging laundry outside a cottage with a bright red door set in an otherwise plain exterior. Aren dismounted. If custom was the same here as in his old hamlet, this woman was the village whore, and probably a rich source of gossip.

"A fine day to you!" she called. "You look thirsty and road weary. Would you care to water your horse and rest yourself for a bit?"

"I would indeed, mistress ...?"

"Nellor." The woman smiled, then turned and hollered over her shoulder. "Koreg!" A boy of about nine summers came running around the side of the cot.

"Yes, Ma?"

"Take the man's horse to the trough, then walk it so it doesn't get stiff."

The boy nodded to Aren as he took the reins. "I'll take good care of him, sir."

Aren watched carefully for a moment to make sure the boy and Pinter were safe together, but the boy clearly had managed horses before.

"I'll not be long, mistress."

"Now that's a shame." The woman grinned. "But a man as hale and hearty as you isn't likely to be, I'd guess. I'd be happy to take my time with someone like you, though. Come inside, and I'll see to your needs while Koreg sees to your mount."

The woman seemed friendly enough but Aren felt no inclination to accept her offer. Still, that was no reason to be impolite. "Nay, mistress, though the thought is tempting, I'm here on the Jarl's business and cannot tarry. What I need most from you is information."

The woman sighed a bit wistfully, but she speared him with a sharp look. "My time is still valuable, however you use it."

Aren dug a half-kron from his belt pouch, no doubt twice what she usually earned of an evening, and held it up. "So is mine, mistress."

The woman nodded. "What information do you seek?"

"What do you know of the women Annikke and Benoia?"

Nellor's eyes narrowed. "You say you're here on the Jarl's business?"

"Aye."

"Not Lord Tholvar's?"

Aren indicated the swooping hawk embroidered on the left breast of his tunic. "I serve Lord Dahleven."

"And what does a Jarl want with two women from our little village?"

"It's not for the likes of me, or you, to question a Jarl's motives."

"Then it's not likely that the 'likes of me' could have aught of value to say to the likes of you or the Jarl is it?"

Aren saw he'd misstepped. "Lord Tholvar brought a complaint against Benoia on behalf of his son Sveyn, but it will be the Jarl who decides what merit that complaint holds and what's to be done about it."

The woman chewed on that for a moment, considering. "What do you want to know?"

"Only the truth as you know it, mistress. What do you know of Annikke and Benoia?"

"There are some as still fear Annikke's silver hair, but I've never seen that she's any different since that

49

summer she was marked. Quieter maybe, but not crazed. She and that girl of hers, they play no favorites. They willingly heal the likes of me and my son as much as they do anyone."

"As long as you can pay," Aren suggested.

"Nay. The two of them sell their herbs in the market, but they heal as needed. They'll accept a chicken or eggs as offered, they have to eat after all, same as anyone, but Annikke asks nothing of those who are ailing."

"And those that annoy them?"

The woman snorted in derision. "What stories is Sveyn telling? If Benoia slapped him, it was no more than he deserved. He's a randy one, and not familiar with, 'No.'"

"He's had trouble before?"

"Trouble? Not him. No one makes trouble for Lord Tholvar's son. Not if they're wise. Some of the girls that serve in his house, now, *they* might be said to have had trouble."

Aren nodded and flipped the half-kron to the woman. "My thanks, mistress."

She caught it handily, and grinned, revealing a gap where a tooth was missing. "Stop by again, sir, when you've more time. I can be generous with my hospitality."

A collection of dry-stacked stone cottages and tradesmen's shops comprised the small village that clustered at the base of the hill upon which Lord Tholvar's house stood. Aren wore Lord Dahleven's livery, so he drew the interest of all who saw him pass.

Aren didn't draw his horse to a stop until he'd reached the blacksmith's shop on the far side of the vil-

lage. Mistress Nellor had told him that she knew no ill of
Annikke or Benoia. Indeed, they had set her boy's arm
the year before with nary a sneer at how Nellor earned
their keep. While some in the village were still wary of
the Fey-marked woman and her servant, and few would
call them friends, her herb craft was well known and
they called upon Annikke when they were ill or injured.
The smithy's wife had been helped most recently by the
herbalist, as had Lord Tholvar's dairyman, and she'd
given Aren directions to both.

The smith thrust a horseshoe into the coals, and
wiped sweat from his brow with a muscular forearm as
Aren dismounted beyond the heat of the forge. "Ye're far
from the Jarl's holdings, sir. What brings ye here?"

"The Jarl has sent me to find your herbalist, Mistress Annikke, and her servant Benoia."

The smithy frowned. "Aye?"

"Aye. Do you know where I might find them?"

"Their cottage can be found down the next track to
the left, sir."

"But they're not there, are they?"

"I wouldn't know. I haven't seen Benoia since two
days past. Longer for Mistress Annikke."

Clearly, the smith wasn't the talkative sort. Aren
tried a different tack. "I should congratulate you. I understand you have a fine new son."

A sudden smile brightened the smith's face. "Aye!
He's a big and lusty one, too."

"And your wife? She's well, I hope?"

"Thanks to Mistress Annikke and her girl. They
helped my Elin. Stayed with her through two long days
of hard labor and saw her safely delivered. So I must ask
you, sir, what does the Jarl seek them for? While I'd not
second guess the Jarl, I'd not be happy to see harm be-
fall those two."

"Harm?" A passing man stopped and lowered his

handcart. The sour smell of drink wafted from him as he leaned against the shed support. "That Fey-spawn deserves what harm she earns."

"And you are?" Aren asked the newcomer.

"I'm the girl's father, who that Annikke stole from me."

"Who you sold, you mean," the smith said.

"Benoia is Annikke's thrall?" Aren asked.

The smith jerked his head in what Aren took to be reluctant assent. "Treated her more like a daughter, though. More than Fornos there did." He lifted his chin, indicating the other man.

"What do you know of the matter? Wait till that squalling babe of yours gets older. You'll learn a thing or two then about raising children." Benoia's father spat into the dust of the street and pushed his handcart filled with wood over to a low building with a thatched roof, muttering to himself all the way about ungrateful daughters and meddlesome neighbors.

chapter eight

ARen found Annikke's cottage without difficulty, thanks to the Smith's directions. It sat alone at the end of a long track that wended deep into the woods. Only one other path split off, but the smith's directions had been clear, and Aren didn't veer from the main trail, though he paused briefly where the two tracks came together. Rain had washed away all sign, but his Talent told him that the women had traveled that other way more recently than the path to the village.

The cottage looked like a thousand others. Grey stones had been dry set, the gaps chinked with moss. Unlike most, the turf roof sported a collection of wildflowers like a colorful bonnet and a long wide porch supported by peeled logs spanned the front. Off to the right of the cottage half a dozen chickens scratched in the herb garden. The whole sat in the center of a wide clearing surrounded by forest. It looked as though the mistress of this domain might step out the door at any moment to toss the wash water, but to Aren it felt empty. The soul of the place was gone.

Aren dismounted, tied Pinter to the rail, and went inside. Broken crockery testified to a hasty departure, or perhaps a careless search. The hearth was cold, its fire burned down to grey ash. The cot in the corner and the bed in the alcove had both been stripped of their blankets. The women were not coming back.

Aren went back outside to walk around the building, going first to the garden. Two rows looked to be planted with vegetables, the rest in herbs. He knelt there. This was Annikke's livelihood. A place she nurtured and depended on. He traced the tender shoots, surprised to find their growth so far advanced for the season. His Tandra had the Talent of nurturing plants, but not so strong.

Was this Annikke's Talent? Or Benoia's?

No matter. Aren rose and continued his circuit of the cottage. On the other side he found the way they'd taken. The rain had obliterated any mark, but his Talent put him on their trail. He knew exactly where they'd slipped into the trackless forest, hoping to elude pursuit.

Aren mounted his horse and followed.

Late afternoon light slanted through the trees as Annikke and Benoia crested a rise near the end of the day. Annikke lifted a hand to shade her eyes to survey the terrain. What she saw made her heart fall.

"Odin's Eye!"

Before them a deep cleft cut across the landscape like a giant furrow plowed by the gods, disappearing into the forest in both directions. Only a bird could cross something like that.

Benoia groaned and sat on the rocky hillside, letting her carry sacks rest beside her.

Annikke knew the general direction Quartzholm lay in, but not the terrain. She'd never left her village, nor seen a map of the area. That ignorance would now cost them precious time. She'd avoided the road on purpose, not wanting to make it easy for Lord Tholvar's men to intercept them. Now they'd have to either go far out of their way to cross the Rift at the lowlands near the Nuvinland river, or back-track to the road, putting them at risk of discovery. Either way held risks. All they could hope was that Tholvar's men wouldn't be looking for them this far from the village.

"We'll rest here," Annikke said to the girl already sitting on the ground. Annikke's bones ached from hiking over rock-strewn terrain and sleeping on the unforgiving ground.

Benoia shook her head and scrambled back to her feet. "No. We need to find a thicket to conceal us. And water."

Annikke nodded. Their water-skins were growing light. "Lead on, then. My choices haven't served us well."

Benoia's head came around. "You got us out of the cottage so Tholvar's men didn't find us that first morn. It's not your fault that your Talent isn't Pathfinding."

Annikke's throat tightened at hearing the girl's staunch defense, but she waved it off. "Even a blind hog can find a truffle now and then."

Benoia's lips thinned, but all she said was, "Let's try this way."

Aren's keen observational skills were of little use to him as he followed the women's trail into the forest. All that led him was his Talent, that *knowing* where a person or animal had gone. His Talent had its limitations. He couldn't *Find* his quarry; he had to *follow*, though if he encountered two intersecting tracks he knew which was the most recent. His Talent had emerged in his thirteenth summer and it had served him well, along with the hunting skills he'd also learned, to feed his family after his father had become an Oathbreaker. No one in their village would do business with such a man. Shamed, his father had packed a carry sack one day and left the responsibility of providing for his family to Aren.

Having touched Annikke's belongings and the seedlings in her garden, Aren had a sense for the woman. He knew Benoia's feel, too, but the cottage was Annikke's and his understanding of her was stronger. He didn't think the women would separate, given what Nellor and the smith had said of them. They'd painted a picture of an isolated woman shunned by most, except when they needed her healing skills. Aren knew what that kind of isolation felt like. Many in his old village would look past him unless he had venison or pelts to trade, not willing to see him as any more trustworthy than his father.

Annikke may have purchased Benoia's service, but she treated the girl more like a daughter, or so the smith had said. Finding one would be as good as finding the other.

Aren paused beside an oak thicket. They'd tarried there a long while, probably that first night. It wasn't very far inside the forest. Why hadn't Lord Tholvar's men seen them? The cover wasn't that good.

He continued on, moving quickly, guided by his Talent, stopping only briefly to rest his mount, dig out journey-bread, or by necessity, when the light fled completely. His Talent would have guided him even in the dark, but it wouldn't protect him from turning an ankle.

The next day was much the same. The women were heading northwest, roughly in the direction of Quartzholm, following the downward slope of the land. Odd. And misguided. They would run into the Rift if they didn't turn aside.

Late in the afternoon he began to see signs of the women's passage. Drifts of disturbed needles. A rock overturned. He was gaining ground on them as they tired. He'd probably catch up with them tomorrow morn. Again he stayed on their trail until dark made continuing too risky. As the last light faded, Aren saw to his mount's needs, and then made another meal of foul-tasting journey-bread before rolling himself in his cloak and falling into a light sleep.

The nearly full moon had passed its zenith, casting the forest in slanting black and silver when Aren awoke. Stars sparkled overhead between the tall trees and the crisp mountain air was still. Too still. He sat up abruptly, reaching for his dagger, and saw that he wasn't alone.

An Elf dressed in leathers stood limned in moonlight not ten feet away, a recurve bow in one hand, and a brace of rabbits dangling from the other.

"Torlon," Aren named the Elf. It had been half a lifetime since the Fey lord had saved him from a charging bear with an arrow loosed from that same bow, but Aren remembered him clearly despite the intervening years. A meeting with the Fey wasn't easy to forget.

Torlon lifted the rabbits. "I brought dinner."

For a moment Aren wondered if he were dreaming. He awoke sweating at least once a year from nightmares about a giant bear charging him, its foul breath hot on his face, its tooth-filled jaws about to crush his skull. In truth, the bear had indeed been huge, but it hadn't come so close. Torlon's arrow had sprouted from the beast's eye before it could eviscerate Aren with its finger length claws. But in Aren's fear-drenched dreams, Torlon was sometimes too slow.

Aren blinked. Torlon was indeed here, not a figment of dream or nightmare. Though miles away from the place of their previous encounter, Aren's one-time rescuer was matter-of-factly offering to share the fruits of his hunt.

"More like breakfast," Aren said, gauging how far gone the night was. He set about clearing the ground and building a fire ring.

Torlon crouched and began cleaning the rabbits. "As you say."

Another Elf came silently through the wood bearing deadwood and joined them, setting his armload down next to Aren. He sat beside Torlon and began gutting the second rabbit.

Torlon gestured with his knife. "This is my brother, Gaelon. Gaelon, this is Dances-with-Bears, otherwise known as Aren."

Gaelon chuckled, nodded to Aren, and then continued with his task.

Aren winced at Torlon's joke, but if Gaelon knew the story, he didn't seem to hold Aren in contempt for his indebtedness. Then again, Elves didn't hold mortals in much esteem anyway, so he wasn't sure the distinction was meaningful. He looked from one brother to the other. The two Elves looked much the same, but they also wore their glamour, so their appearance was no proof they were related. "While the rabbits are welcome, I already ate."

The new Elf made a face. "Journey-bread."

They know what I had for supper? "You've been *watching* me?"

"Yes."

How often had the Fey observed him while he hunted? The thought was disturbing, but had Torlon not been close at hand that time years ago, Aren would be dead. Nonplussed, all Aren could think to say was, "I would have gladly shared my meal with you."

"Kindly meant, I'm sure, but only the desperate would consider journey-bread food."

Aren laughed. "True, but it packs light, and it's sustaining."

Torlon spitted the rabbits and propped them over the growing flames. "Starvation might be preferable."

As the rabbits cooked they talked of hunting and harvests and weather, all matters essential to people living close to the land, and nothing important enough to merit a visit from the Fey.

The sky was showing the first kiss of dawn when Torlon threw the last of the now clean bones into the fire. Gaelon pulled a metal pot from his pack, filled it with water from a skin, then threw leaves into it. As the water heated, it released a lovely aroma. Aren forced himself to relax. He hadn't asked any questions of the Elves, but they must have a reason to be here, with him. They would speak when they were ready. At any other time this would pleasant, though strange. But now that the sky was growing pale, it was time for him to be off.

When the water came to a simmer, Gaelon produced three cups. It was light enough to see that they were beautifully wrought, with rolled gold at the edges and delicate scrollwork carved down the handles. Not what Aren would think was typical camping gear. The Elf carefully poured the tea and handed the cups around, then saluted with his before drinking. "To Freyr and Freya. May they bless you and your herds, and increase your family."

"To Freyr and Freya," Aren echoed. "May they reward your generosity for this meal. It was indeed better than journey-bread."

Torlon sipped his tea. "Now it's time for talk. I have come to collect on your debt."

Aren nodded, hiding a stab of alarm. He owed this Fey his life. Whatever Torlon asked, Aren would do if it were in his power, but what would the Elf require, that he couldn't do for himself?

"You are following Annikke and Benoia. Why?"

Aren lifted his brows, surprised at the Elves interest in his mission, and further surprised that they knew by name the women he was tracking. "The Jarl has tasked me with bringing them to Quartzholm."

"Why?"

Aren saw no reason to hide the truth, and suspected it would be useless to try in any case. "Lord Tholvar has accused Benoia of a crime, and Annikke of aiding her escape. I'm to bring them to Lord Dahleven so that he may sort out the matter."

"We know of Dahleven, but who is this Tholvar?" Torlon asked.

Aren shook his head. "I have no direct experience of the man. Only rumor." But that rumor wasn't good.

"It's of no consequence," Gaelon said, waving a hand dismissively. "I ask that you return to Quartzholm, and leave the women to our protection."

"I cannot. I've sworn to serve Lord Dahleven."

Torlon exchanged a look with his brother. "You would not have lived to swear that oath had I not saved your life," he said softly.

Aren's heart clenched in dread. What the Elf said was true. He was cross-sworn, and his debt to Torlon preceded his oath to Lord Dahleven.

He looked at Torlon. It was to him that he owed his debt, not Gaelon. "Is this what *you* ask of me?"

Torlon finished his tea, then flung the dregs into

the fire. A spurt of steam sizzled and rose into the air. The Elf held his empty cup in both hands, staring into it as if reading the leaves. After a moment he raised his head and his pale, un-glamoured eyes met Aren's.

"I ask that you protect Annikke and do all in your power to see that no grief befalls her. Then your debt will be repaid."

"What you ask is impossible!" Aren exclaimed. "No mortal can spare another from all grief! I doubt even you could do so."

Torlon cast an inscrutable look at his brother. "True enough. But as you owe your life to my intervention, I ask that you intervene to protect Annikke until she is home again and safe, and bring her no grief. Can you do *that*?"

Aren bowed his head. What the Elf asked of him was possible. But if he did it, all his efforts to erase the taint that his father had brought upon the family would be for naught. He was cross-sworn, and Aren could see no honorable way to sidestep it. He owed his miserable life to the Elf. If he took Benoia to meet Lord Tholvar's justice, he would bring Annikke grief. If he did not, Lord Dahleven would name him Oathbreaker.

"So be it."

chapter nine

JUST BEFORE DAWN, Annikke awoke to Benoia shaking her.

"Do you smell that?" Benoia asked.

Annikke blinked, trying to clear the fog from her head and sat up. She sniffed. Pine and leaf mold dominated, but very faintly the scent of wood smoke came lilting on the breeze. And something else. She sniffed again. Was that meat cooking? Her stomach rumbled. She and Benoia had kept cold camps since they'd left their cottage to avoid drawing attention. All they'd had to eat for the last three days were shriveled apples, stale bread, and cheese.

She forced herself to concentrate. *Now is not the time to be thinking of food.*

"The smell is faint, but still too close. We're far from any homestead or village."

"The wind follows our path," Benoia said. "It's those men. The ones who were following us."

"It could be hunters." Annikke countered. *Or*

Elves.

Fear banished the last wisps of fog from Annikke's brain. She shivered at the thought of meeting them again.

"How likely is that?" Benoia asked.

The girl was right, and wishful thinking wouldn't make it so. Only their pursuers were likely to be this deep into the forest. If Tholvar's men were close enough on their heels that she and Benoia could smell the smoke from their fire, they were nearly caught.

"We have to move. Now."

Benoia was already packing their carry-sacks and rolling up their blankets.

They'd walked beside the cleft for a day, following it downhill, toward the Nuvinland river. It wasn't the shortest path to Quartzholm, but it led away from the road where Annikke was sure Tholvar's men would have been looking for them. Now it seemed that taking the indirect route had done them no good.

Annikke took the bundles that Benoia held out to her, slung them across her shoulders and set out at as brisk a pace as she could manage in the fading starlight. There was an eerie familiarity to the forest, and she shivered. She still didn't recollect exactly where the Elves had taken her so long ago, even with her memory restored. Were they close to the Elvenholt here?

A sudden feeling of yearning stabbed her breast, followed quickly by dread. She couldn't go there again. She knew in her bones that if she did, she'd never be able to leave that intoxicating beauty. The life she'd built for herself and Benoia would be over. That life might well be past now anyway, thanks to Sveyn, but as hard as it was, this was *her* life. Hers and Benoia's.

Annikke pushed on even faster once golden light gilded the tops of the trees. The sound of the stream running with snow-melt echoed from the bottom of the ravine, white water cutting the cleft ever deeper as it raced to the river. As the elevation declined, the forest changed. Pines gave way to oak and aspen, trees that dropped their leaves each winter and reclothed themselves in the spring. Now that it was early summer their branches were full and bright with new growth and the forest floor sprouted grasses and wildflowers. All around them the forest thrummed with life.

Too much life, Annikke grumbled to herself as the thick grass and undergrowth dragged at their skirts, slowing their progress.

The flowing, wide-legged split skirts they wore quickly grew damp to the knees with dew. Annikke looked behind them when they stopped to catch their breath, and groaned with dismay. The rising sun slanted through the tree trunks, revealing their path. Crushed grass and wildflowers swept clear of moisture clearly showed the way she and Benoia had traveled. They might as well have built a cairn, marking their trail.

"Follow me," she said, as she turned back the way they'd come.

"Where are we going?" Benoia asked, fear in her tone.

"We're leaving too much sign. Let's make it work for us."

Annikke retraced their path, losing half a candle-mark's worth of travel, and then veered off at an angle. After going only a few strides, she knelt to sweep her hand over the bent plants and murmur words of encouragement. Slowly the stems and leaves straightened, seeking the sun. She couldn't do anything about the dew their skirts swept up, but soon the rising warmth would dry the beads of moisture clinging to every leaf and stem and the path she and Benoia had taken would look no different than the rest of the forest floor.

"With a little luck, whoever is following will continue on the way we were going," Annikke said.

"Won't they figure it out when our trail suddenly stops?" Benoia asked.

"Yes. But they'll spend some time looking for our true direction, I hope. That may buy us some time."

But not enough. They'd left no trail in the pine needles. The initial pursuit had given up only a short way into the forest. Whoever was following them now had picked up their track sometime later. They should be more than half a day behind—and yet they weren't. Their pursuers must be guided by a Finder or Tracker Talent, though where Lord Tholvar had found one of those Annikke couldn't imagine. Such Talents weren't common, and he had none in his service. She could only hope that her little subterfuge would slow them a little.

"Time for what?" Benoia asked.

What indeed?

They continued on, at an angle away from the direction they'd been going before, but before Annikke could think of an answer to her foster-daughter's question, they had to stop so Annikke could use her Talent again. The effect didn't extend very far, and she had to stop often to whisper words of health and vigor to the plants to help them stand tall.

The third time Annikke stopped, Benoia said, "This is slowing us down too much. If we tarry much more, they won't have to find our trail. They'll be able to see us!"

The girl was right. Annikke stared at the short distance they'd come, and then forward into the undergrowth. A plan began to form. "We're not trying to outrun our pursuit."

"We're not?"

"Our pursuers haven't been slowed by searching for our trail, they're traveling at speed." Annikke straightened and put a hand on Benoia's shoulder. "We can't outpace long-legged men in any case. After we put a bit more distance behind us, we'll find a thicket to hide in, then ask it to conceal us until whoever follows us gives up their search here. If those hunting us are Finders of people, we're as good as caught, but Lord Tholvar has no such Talents in his employ. If they are Trackers of only minor Talent, my subterfuge may work."

Benoia's face twisted. Clearly she was impatient to hurry on. "All right. How can I help?"

A familiar warmth filled Annikke's heart. Benoia had ever been willing to offer assistance when needed, even when she'd first come into Annikke's care and Annikke had been slow to give the love the girl so needed.

"Go on ahead and find a thicket we can hide in. I'll follow as quick as I may."

Benoia frowned, but nodded, then set off in the direction Annikke indicated.

Annikke followed slowly, whispering to the wildflowers to obscure her trail, quite confident Benoia would not be happy with the next part of her plan.

The sun was high overhead when Aren stopped, staring at the bent stalks of wildflowers ahead, then into the unmarked undergrowth to his left. The path ahead was unmistakable, and his Talent told him that they had indeed passed this way. And yet his Talent also told him that they'd gone deeper into the forest, moving away from the ravine. Annikke and Benoia had gone in both directions. Up until now, they hadn't done anything to hide their trail. Doing so hadn't been necessary under the pines. All they'd had to do there was avoid scuffing their feet too much. Perhaps they'd realized they were leaving sign and begun to cover their tracks as a precaution.

Or maybe they'd become aware they were being followed.

The more recent path was the more obscure one. Aren veered into the unmarked undergrowth.

Guided only by his Talent, Aren confidently led his horse past an aspen grove on his right, then came abreast of a thicket of young oaks surrounding a pair of old trees with gnarled bark and spreading boughs. The women were close. He could feel that they hadn't passed this way very long ago. The hunting skills he'd honed after his father fled helped him notice immediately when the wildflowers began showing signs of someone passing through again. Had the women grown careless, confident that they'd shaken their pursuit?

He looked closer. No. This was another trick. They'd split up. While there were no visible signs marking their path, Annikke and Benoia had both gone toward the oak thicket, but only Benoia had stayed. Annikke had laid a clear trail to draw pursuit away from the girl much the same way a woodcock hen would flutter to distract a predator from her chicks.

Aren walked over to the tangle of weedy saplings and undergrowth and stared into the shadowed thicket. If he captured Benoia, he'd soon have Annikke in hand as well. She wouldn't let her servant face Lord Dahleven's justice alone. Then, he need only escort them to Quartzholm.

Simple. Except he'd promised Torlon that he would protect Annikke and bring her no grief.

Taking Benoia to Quartzholm would very likely bring Annikke grief if she cared for her servant as much as he'd come to believe. Why else would she have left her home to aid the younger woman's escape from Thorvald?

He could walk away. He could tell Lord Fender

that he'd been unable to Track Benoia.

But leaving the women to wander the forest alone wouldn't keep them safe, and just the thought of dissembling to Lord Fender made him want to vomit.

That falsehood would mark him an incompetent. And not only would that undermine Lord Dahleven's confidence in him, but it would be a lie. A lie the Jarl's brother, Father Ragnar, the Overprest, would effortlessly detect. Aren would be an Oathbreaker, and no better than his father. He couldn't do that to his daughter.

He found the place the women had entered the thicket. The saplings showed no evidence of being bent or broken, yet they stood so close together even a slender girl would have had to force them apart to slide between. This along with the proof of the wildflowers, and Annikke's herb garden, made him certain one or the other had a Talent with plants.

"Benoia!" Aren lifted his voice. "I mean you no harm, but you must come back to Quartzholm with me. The Jarl commands it."

As he expected, all he heard in response was the humming of insects and a distant bird chirping.

"I can drag you out of there, but I'd rather not. You cannot outrun me, or hide from me. Let's make this easy on us both."

Again there was no reply to his request. Aren sighed. This reminded him forcefully of when Tandra had hidden from him after breaking her grandmother's best crockery bowl. Except the consequences to Benoia would probably be much more severe than extra chores and no honey on her bread for a week.

His vow to protect Annikke meant he had to protect Benoia as well.

Nevertheless, he couldn't walk away.

Aren tied his horse to a sapling, and then shouldered his way into the dimness of the thicket, pushing aside twiggy growth clustered with leaves. "Benoia," he called again. Two steps in, the branches twisted around his legs and arms, stopping all progress.

Alarm shot through Aren as the young trees crowded him. He hadn't seen them move, but they pressed closer than they should. He raised one arm forcefully. Twiglets caught at his sleeves, scratching and stabbing with every movement. He would have to do real damage to the plants, and to himself, to win free.

chapter ten

ANNIKKE CAUTIOUSLY APPROACHED the hunter from behind, stopping a few paces from where the thicket held him fast.

It had been an amazing bit of good fortune that this man was alone. She'd first planned to hide Benoia and lead those hunting them away from her. She and her foster-daughter would reunite downstream at the ferry landing, and if Annikke didn't show in three days' time, she'd commanded her foster daughter to seek out the Daughters of Freya in Forsvaremur. Lord Fender's debt was to Annikke, and if she couldn't call upon him, the Daughters were Benoia's next best chance.

Benoia had fiercely refused at first, but she'd had no better idea. So Annikke had laid a trail any fool could follow away from the thicket, and obscured all sign that Benoia hid among the young saplings.

But the man hadn't been a fool, and hadn't followed her false trail. He was clearly a Tracker Talent of considerable skill, because he'd headed straight for the stand of young oaks and his quarry.

He might not be a fool, but he *was* alone. Another plan blossomed. If she could stop his pursuit, they might still have a chance.

Benoia had somehow reversed the healing magic the Elves had given them in a fit of panic. Perhaps Annikke could do the same and lame the man enough to slow him, allowing them to get away. They'd have to steal his horse, too, or he'd just ride after them, but what was theft, even of a valuable animal, when you planned to maim a man?

Annikke lifted her hand. Hesitated. She'd never harmed someone before. Before she even had magic the villagers had feared her Fey-marking. With this choice, all the years she'd carefully cultivated her neighbors' trust would be as naught. Their fear of her, of her Fey-marking, would be justified.

She had to do this. He wasn't struggling yet, but the young oaks didn't have the strength to hold him for long, and if they tried to, he'd soon tear them to pieces trying to free himself. Benoia's future depended on this. Annikke didn't want to think of what Lord Tholvar would do to her foster-daughter if she fell into his hands.

Only now that their pursuer was caught and within reach, she couldn't do it. She was certainly frightened enough for her foster-daughter. That alone should have given her the strength to follow through. But the man wasn't offering them immediate injury. He wasn't even thrashing and fighting the plants.

He turned his head, and looked at her over his shoulder. His eyes widened, and he hesitated a moment before saying, "Let me loose, mistress Annikke. I'll not harm you or the girl."

"Ha!" Annikke exclaimed. Did the man think her silver hair meant she was simple-minded? "Don't lie.

Lord Tholvar will sell her as a thrall—*if* she survives the flogging he'll give her."

"Then it's good that it wasn't Lord Tholvar who sent me. I am Aren Birgirsson, in service to Lord Fendrikanin of Quartzholm."

Annikke drew back her hand as surprise rippled through her. "Lord Fender sent you? Why?"

"He wants to make sure you're treated justly. He said he owes you a debt."

Hope flared in Annikke's heart, and doubt alongside it. "What can he do? Lord Tholvar is a powerful man. Only the Jarl might counter him, and that's but a tenuous hope."

"It was the Jarl who sent me, mistress." The man moved slowly, gradually easing one tangled arm free and folding it close to his chest.

Annikke laughed bitterly as her hope died. The man was piling lie upon falsehood. "Do I look so gullible? You don't even know Lord Fendrikanin, do you? The Jarl has no reason to take any interest in the likes of me and my foster-daughter."

"Lord Tholvar gave him reason. Tholvar's men searched for you, but lost you in the forest. He has no Tracker Talents able to find you so he asked the Jarl for aid. *He* made you Lord Dahleven's business. It will be Lord Dahleven who decides your fate and that of your servant, not Tholvar. And Lord Fender has the Jarl's ear." Aren gently pulled his other arm free. "Quartzholm is the safest place for you now."

Could what he was saying be true?

Lord Fender's debt to her had been Annikke's hope when she'd dragged Benoia into the forest. A hope that had seemed thin at best. She wanted to believe this man, but did she dare? If she chose wrong, her foster-daughter's life would be destroyed.

Benoia appeared at her side and clutched at her

arm. "Why are you talking? We've got to go!"

Annikke let Benoia pull her away a step, then another. She had no reason to trust this man. And Tholvar could only be trusted to vent his anger upon Benoia and Annikke both. Benoia went to Aren's horse and untied the reins. Annikke couldn't bring herself to lame the man, but she and Benoia might be able to outpace him if they rode and he was on foot.

"Lord Fender is an honorable man, mistress." Aren said. "He pays his debts."

Annikke hesitated. Lord Fender had given them courtesy five years ago, even though he could clearly see she was Fey-marked. He'd even tried to protect her on that long ago night. She put her hand on Benoia's wrist. "Wait."

Benoia turned wide, frightened eyes up to her. Annikke caught a glimpse of the beaten girl that had been sold into her service in those eyes, and she hated Sveyn for what he'd tried to do. For the hundredth time, Annikke wished it had been she who'd been caught in the forest, and not Benoia. She'd have done more than shrivel his miserable little cock.

"I'll not let any man harm you," Annikke said.

"You can't stop them!" Benoia shot back. "Men do as they will, with none to gainsay them!"

Annikke turned back to Aren. "Let my daughter go. Take me to Quartzholm. I'll take her punishment."

"No!" Benoia protested. "It was my fault!"

"Don't you ever think that! What happened is on Sveyn's head," Annikke answered. "You only defended yourself."

Benoia looked away.

"What happened, mistress?" Aren asked gently.

"What do you think? A lord's son thought anything, or anyone he saw was his for the taking, including my daughter." Annikke pulled Benoia into a fierce hug.

There was no shame in young folk sharing the pleasures of their bodies, but it should be just that, a sharing. Not a violent, forceful *taking* of something not freely offered. She wanted better memories for Benoia than that. Better memories than Annikke had. Tears tracked her cheeks, but she paid them no mind. If the man thought her weak, he'd soon learn differently.

Aren turned his upper body to face the women. "I'm sorry. It's clear to me that Sveyn was in the wrong, and it will be clear to Lord Dahleven as well, I'm sure."

"He's a lord!" Annikke scoffed. "And lords stick together."

"The Jarl is a fair man. He will deal honestly with you, if you're honest with him."

"You know the Jarl so well as that, do you, that you can speak for him?" Annikke didn't try to conceal her derision. "I think it more likely that you'd say anything to make us compliant. A handsome fellow like you no doubt expects to get whatever you want from women. A few honeyed words and they just drop into your hand. *I* will not."

The man laughed, and it was a bitter sound. "Mistress Annikke, you're right. I cannot speak for the Jarl. But I do not believe Lord Fendrikanin would serve a man so unjust that he would punish a woman wrongfully accused. If you do not come back with me, and you elude me, some other man will be sent to hunt you. You will never be able to rest. What life is that for the girl?"

Annikke pressed her lips tightly together, unhappy that he'd given her own argument back to her. She stood there, still holding Benoia, with the girl's arms still wrapped around her, and tried to think of some other way. She couldn't find one, no more than she'd been able to for the last few days. "He's right, girl," she said softly as the horse tossed its head, tugging the reins. Benoia stepped out of Annikke's embrace to keep control of the beast.

Benoia lifted a tear stained face, but her expression was fierce. "Then it should be me who goes to Quartzholm. You're not responsible. I don't want them to blame you for what I did. You should go home to our cottage."

"And let you face Tholvar and Sveyn by yourself? No." Annikke put her hands on Benoia's cheeks and smiled even though she felt like crying too. She wiped the girl's tears away with her thumbs. "I won't let them separate us. You'll not face this alone," she murmured.

Then she turned and reached into the thicket, holding out her hand to their captor.

Aren took Annikke's hand, gently wrapping his fingers around hers. As he did, the saplings that held his legs no longer restrained him. Her hand was warm and strong, but he read the promise in her eyes: *Bring harm to my daughter and I'll have your skin.*

She'd have to get in line. The Elves had made no specific threats if he didn't protect Annikke, but he didn't doubt there would be consequences if he failed to pay his debt. Beyond that, his honor wouldn't allow him to shirk his obligation. How he would fulfill both his debt to Torlon and his duty to Lord Dahleven, he didn't yet know.

Benoia glared at him and gave him a wide berth. The young woman was small and slender, and looked younger than her seventeen summers. She held herself rigidly, with lifted chin and squared shoulders. He thought of his own daughter, Tandra, and recognized that Benoia was struggling to maintain a tenuous self-control.

Aren wouldn't challenge her. He had no way of knowing the truth of the matter, beyond the gossip he'd gathered, but if half of what he'd heard about Sveyn was true, Benoia deserved to keep what dignity she could. Had someone treated Tandra with the disrespect that Sveyn had apparently shown Benoia, he'd have seen the young lord lying scattered in pieces. He scowled at the thought, and Benoia flinched.

"What now?" Annikke asked.

Aren looked at the Fey-marked woman. Fatigue and worry shadowed her eyes and there was a smudge on her cheek that he wanted to reach out and wipe away. Her glorious silver hair was coming loose from a braid that hung down to her waist. Falling free, he could imagine that tips of those strands would tease her nicely rounded rear. He would enjoy brushing those silver locks.

"Will you tie us up and drag us behind your horse?"

Annikke's blunt question shook him free of his inappropriate thoughts.

Aren looked at the sun's position, gauging the time left in the day. Should they travel a distance to burn off some of the fight the women still had in them, or give them a respite to get used to him first? Aren looked from one to the other. He'd been on their trail since dawn with no break. He suspected they'd taken none, either.

"I haven't eaten since before daylight," he said. "Shall we break our fast before we continue?"

Annikke and Benoia exchanged a glance, then Annikke nodded.

The day's eye was past zenith and the afternoon had grown warm, so they tucked themselves into the dappled shadows from one of the taller trees. Aren loosened the cinch on Pinter's saddle and picketed her in a patch of meadow grass. The women shared nuts and a chunk of yellow cheese between them. Aren dug out a hunk of journey-bread and a bit of jerked venison.

They ate in silence. Aren watched the women, and the women watched him back, not even trying to pretend they weren't.

Aren finished his portion before Annikke and Benoia did theirs, but he saw no point in rushing them. They had candlemarks of sunlight left, and since the women had traveled away from the closest road to Quartzholm, it would take at least two days to backtrack through the forest to the road.

"What's Quartzholm like?" Benoia asked.

The girl's question surprised Aren. He hadn't thought she would speak to him directly. "It's big. Magnificent, actually. The outer walls are granite, but much of the castle is rose quartz. Great Talents crafted it before Fanlon's time, so the walls are smooth and seamless except where Talents have carved scenes of beauty into the stone. It's a bit of a maze, and it's easy to get lost among the many halls and staircases. Outside the wall, there's a village that surrounds the castle and flows down the hillside."

Benoia nodded and bit her lips.

Aren realized that what she really wanted to know was, *What will happen to us there?* So he continued as if she'd spoken the words. "After we pass through the gates, I'll escort you to Lord Fender. I expect he'll arrange for you to bathe and eat before you go before Lord Dahleven, but if he doesn't, I will." Whatever they'd done, for whatever reason, they deserved that courtesy.

Benoia's brows rose in either surprise or skepticism, he couldn't tell. He didn't think she was aware of breathing the words, "A bath," with apparent longing.

A smile played at the edges of Annikke's mouth. Had she needed to wrestle Benoia into the bath when she was younger, as he had his own daughter?

When they'd all finished their meal, Aren tightened the cinch on his horse's saddle and said, "Mistress Annikke, if you mount first, Benoia can ride behind you."

Annikke's brows rose. "*We're* to ride?"

"This beast can easily carry you both."

"No, I mean, you're letting *us* ride?"

Aren tried not to take affront. "I'm no lord to ride while women walk."

"But we're accused of harming a man."

"Accused is not guilty." He gestured for Annikke to come closer to the horse.

"Few would agree with you." Annikke said.

He thought of how the villagers of his youth had turned on his father even before they'd known the truth, how they'd made Aren's life harder because of who his father was. "I won't judge without proof. But I *will* ask you for your parole. I'd rather not have to tie you each night. Swear to me that you will not try to escape, or to injure me in my sleep."

"I swear to accompany you to Quartzholm with complete docility," Annikke said.

Benoia laughed. "Docility? I'll go with you to Quartzholm just to see this wonder."

"Benoia." Aren spoke in the same gruff tone he used to reprove his daughter. "Show Annikke the respect she deserves."

Benoia's expression flashed from outrage to shame before she looked down at her feet. "I beg pardon, Annikke."

"Granted. Now swear your parole."

The young woman lifted her head and met Aren's gaze. "I swear to you that I will neither attempt escape nor will I harm you—unless you try to harm me or Annikke."

Aren nodded to each of the women. "Accepted." He

made a step of his laced fingers. "Annikke?"

She took a step back and looked up. "I've treated horses, but never been on one. It looks very tall."

"But beautiful," Benoia said, petting Pinter's nose. "Is she yours?"

Aren shook his head, standing straight and letting his hands relax by his sides. "On loan to me for this task."

Benoia ran her hand down the mare's neck, admiration in her gaze. "Lord Tholvar and Sveyn ride fine mounts, and Lord Fender had a fine horse, but the only others I've seen are draft animals."

"Pinter has a smooth gait, Annikke, and I'll be leading her. You'll have nothing to fear," Aren said, gently.

Annikke nodded stiffly. "I trust you."

Something twisted deep within him. Aren wanted to look away, but he couldn't break away from her clear blue gaze. She *trusted* him? He was here to take her foster-daughter to judgment. And while he'd sworn to bring her no harm or grief, he wasn't sure if he'd be able to keep his word. He nodded wordlessly and threaded his fingers together again.

Annikke put her foot into his hands. Trust or no, she squeaked as he tossed her into the shallow saddle, and Aren bit his lip to keep from laughing.

She grabbed for a handful of mane to balance herself, then looked down on him. Her eyes were wide with alarm, but they narrowed as she caught his expression. "Is my fear a source of merriment to you?"

There was no good answer to that. The honest answer wasn't the best one. Aren shook his head, and gestured Benoia closer. The girl shared an amused glance with him, then closed her expression as she remembered he was her captor. Aren sighed, and he tossed her up behind Annikke. It was only right that the girl be wary of him, but he wished it could be otherwise.

Benoia put her arms around Annikke, and the older woman relaxed a little.

Aren tied their carry sacks to either side of the saddle, twitched the reins and led them toward Quartzholm.

chapter eleven

A FEW CANDLEMARKS LATER, Annikke's aching arse told her she'd need the liniment she'd packed. Aren had spoken truth: the mare did have a steady gait, and although the ground still seemed to be quite far away, Annikke no longer feared the horse would shy and toss her and Benoia off. In fact, after she'd gotten used to the beast's stride, she rather enjoyed the view from atop its broad back.

They'd turned back to travel up country along the Rift because following it was the shortest way to return to the road, but Aren chose a course well away from the crumbly edge. Despite the rough ground, they'd made decent progress.

The sun was westering when Aren halted the mare, cocking his head and listening. All Annikke heard was the breeze ruffling the new leaves.

"Why are we stopping?" Benoia asked.

Aren didn't answer. He didn't even seem to have heard the question.

Annikke felt Benoia draw breath for another query, but she put a finger to her lips and the girl remained quiet.

Several moments passed before Aren looked around him, almost as if scenting the wind. "Someone passed by here, not long ago."

"Someone?" Annikke asked.

"One of Lord Tholvar's men?" Benoia asked with a slight quaver in her voice.

Annikke squeezed Benoia's hand trying to give some reassurance, though she really had none to offer.

Aren shook his head slowly. "I don't think so."

"Who else would be out here? We're in the middle of nowhere," Benoia argued.

Aren gazed at the ground, covered with leaf litter. "A stripling youth, I think. The stride is a bit short to be a grown man's, but it's longer than most women's. The odd thing is, it wasn't here a hundred paces ago."

"Perhaps you missed it?" Annikke suggested.

Aren's expression appeared somewhat affronted.

Annikke felt her face grow warm as she realized she'd just insulted his Talent. She opened her mouth to apologize, but stopped as Aren barked a laugh and shook his head.

"Indeed." Aren dropped the reins and walked back the way they'd come several paces, then walked an arc, pausing in half a dozen places. He removed another hundred strides farther and followed a similar arc, then trailed another distance along a single line until he was almost out of sight among the trees.

A thought slithered into her mind. Aren was a good distance away and they had the horse. *We could escape.*

She shoved the idea away as soon as it surfaced, ashamed she'd even thought it. *We gave our parole.*

Before she could tempt herself again, she saw Aren striding toward them through the trees.

"A reasonable thought, Mistress Annikke," he said as he took up the lead again, "but, thankfully, my Talent is not in question. The trail comes in at a slight angle." He pointed along the way he'd examined. "There are signs that someone has tried to conceal their passing,"

"But your Talent still reveals it to you?"

"Yes. The trail vanishes completely, but it begins again abruptly, then stops again, and starts up again here." Aren pointed to a spot on the ground. "As if someone was making great leaps."

"I've never heard of such a Talent."

"Nor have I. I'd guess this youth's Talent is some kind of Concealment, and not yet well honed."

"But why would he be *here*?" Benoia asked.

"My Talent only shows me that someone passed this way, not the why."

"Do you think it's someone looking for me?" she asked in a worried tone.

"Unlikely. This boy has been concealing his trail. I cannot think why someone searching for you would do that. He's probably running from someone, just as you were."

"Who would guess the forest would be so crowded?" Annikke muttered.

Aren grinned, and Annikke felt an unfamiliar flutter of pleasure, that he enjoyed her attempt at humor.

"Should we turn away from his path?" Benoia asked. "He might be a criminal. A real one. What if whoever is looking for him finds us, instead?"

Aren shook his head. "This youth seems to be alone, and more likely to avoid us than seek us out. And his pursuers, if there are any, have their own quarry. They won't waste time on us."

"What if he's running from Oathbreakers? What if he *is* an Oathbreaker?" Benoia persisted.

Aren stiffened and his face took on a peculiar expression. "Not all Oathbreakers are bandits, girl." His tone was sharp.

"But—"

"Enough! This is the shortest way. This is the way we're going." Aren turned and tugged on Pinter's lead, clicking his tongue to encourage the horse to follow.

Annikke glared at Aren's back, but didn't waste her breath on a reproof.

I shouldn't have been so hard on the girl, Aren chided himself silently as he trudged along with Pinter and the women following. She'd only spoken a fear that many held. Anyone craven or feckless enough to break a sworn oath was only a step away from thievery or worse. So many believed. But though his father had brought disgrace on his family, Aren could no more imagine him turning to thievery than he would himself. Not all Oathbreakers were dangerous men.

Few saw beyond the dishonor, however. The fact that Oathbreakers were shunned and often had no honest way to fill their bellies, or satisfy the hunger of their loved ones, was a just consequence of their actions. No one looked closer than that.

Aren pushed away the bitter thoughts. His father's actions had no bearing on today's tasks.

Aren led them northwest, on a route calculated to intersect the road to Quartzholm late the next day. The ground rose, and gradually pines began to outnumber oaks and aspen. He took a lazy weaving pattern through the trees, watching for the intermittent trail they'd crossed earlier. The longer he followed, the more he became convinced that they followed someone whose Talent was either weak or poorly trained. Now that Aren knew what he was looking for, he easily found sign of a single person doing his best to leave no trail. Whoever it was had some woodcraft, but Aren's skill as a hunter made it possible for him to follow.

Whoever was ahead of them wasn't experienced at evading pursuit. The fool never changed direction when his Talent obscured the trail. Aren didn't have to search for the track. He just continued on his own path, and soon he'd find the sign resumed several hundred paces onward. That, in addition to the length of the person's stride, reinforced his belief that they were following a callow youth. Someone more experienced would have altered direction while their Talent hid their passage, requiring anyone hunting him to spend time casting about for a new track. Nor would a person serious about avoiding discovery have rested so often.

As the day waned, they gained ground on the other traveler. The sun was low in the sky when Aren called a halt.

"What about the fellow we're following?" Benoia asked. "Shouldn't we keep going? Find out who he is?"

"I don't want to come upon him in the dark," Aren said. *Certainly not with two women in tow.* "He'll have to stop soon as well. We'll catch up with him tomorrow—if we want to." *Though it might be better to remain half a day behind.*

Benoia nodded and jumped down from her perch behind Annikke. Aren reached up to help Annikke. She put her hands on his shoulders and swung a leg over Pinter's withers, but when she hit the ground her legs threatened to give way. Aren tightened his hold. She colored and looked away, but Aren kept his hands on her waist until she steadied. Despite her long trek before he found them, she still smelled of the fragrant herbs that must have scented her bath water. In a flash his mind supplied him with an image of her submerged in a large soaking tub like those in Quartzholm, water lapping at the curve of her breasts.

Annikke dropped her hands from his shoulders, but didn't step away. She couldn't. The horse was at her back. "What are you smiling at?"

Aren cleared his throat and tried without much success to wipe the arousing picture from his imagination. "Just looking forward to the pleasures of a hot bath," he said.

"A bath," Benoia said with a sigh. "How long until we get to Quartzholm?"

A shriek echoed through the forest, silencing the birds and jolting Aren to alert. Whoever had voiced that cry was in trouble.

Aren marked the direction, then turned to his horse, quickly untying the women's packs from the saddle and dropping them at their feet. Whatever this was, it wasn't his business. He had his own responsibilities: to protect Annikke, to bring Benoia to Quartzholm. But he couldn't ignore someone in distress.

"Stay here. I'll be back as soon as I can." He met Annikke's eyes with a direct gaze.

She nodded. "We'll be here." They'd given their parole, after all.

Aren pulled himself into the saddle, then guided the horse toward what was probably going to be a complication he didn't need.

chapter twelve

"LET'S BUILD A FIRE," Annikke said.

"A fire!" Benoia said with delight.

Annikke could sympathize with her foster-daughter's pleasure. They'd clung to each other through the last few nights, fighting the chill of summer nights in the mountains. "We're not hiding any longer. We might as well be warm." Annikke cleared a space and gathered stones for a fire ring while Benoia collected deadfall. Neither one carried an axe to cut wood, nor would they use it on living trees if even if they had. All knew of how the tree-folk had come to Quartzholm's aid.

The light was fading when Annikke heard the heavy sound of the horse's walk muffled by fallen needles and long dead leaves. Aren came into sight soon after, leading Pinter through the evening shadows, with a young man barely clinging to the horse's neck.

"Who is this?" Annikke stood as Aren tethered his horse to a tree.

"This, I believe, is the fellow who's been leaving,

and not leaving, the trail we encountered." Aren said, as he pulled the youth from Pinter's back.

He was halfway to manhood, at that gangly age before he put muscle on bone, which was a good thing since Aren was clearly taking most of his weight. Aren half carried him over to the blanket Annikke had been sitting on, and eased him down.

"What happened?" Benoia asked.

"I wasn't able to get much from him," Aren said. "His name is Vali. He may have hit his head when he slipped down the cliff. Lucky for him, a ledge stopped his descent. Otherwise he'd have fallen all the way down to the river below."

Annikke knelt beside Vali and felt his scalp. "No bumps." She lifted each eyelid. "His eyes appear normal as well." She felt along all of his limbs. "I think his wrist is sprained."

"I thought it looked broken," Aren said.

He was right. The wrist was broken, but a "sprained" wrist wouldn't draw as much attention when it healed unusually fast.

"What's he doing out here?" Benoia asked as she covered Vali with another blanket.

"He didn't say. I could barely rouse him enough to get a rope around him and haul him up the cliff face. If he didn't hit his head, why won't he wake?"

Annikke shared a look with Benoia as she laid a hand on the youth's head. "I don't know, but it's for the best. I can tend his arm and he'll not suffer."

"I'll help you unsaddle Pinter," Benoia said brightly. "Then we'll probably need to gather more wood."

Annikke waited while Aren turned to tend his horse. She put her fingers over the young man's arm and, with a quick glance over her shoulder to make sure Aren wasn't watching, called on the Elven magic Gaelon had gifted her. Her hands grew warm as she murmured the beautiful Elven words.

A wave of vertigo made the earth tilt a bit, but it passed quickly since the bone hadn't been displaced, and it didn't take much to start it knitting. This was the price she paid for using the Elf's gift. She hadn't been able to stand for a candlemark after healing Lord Thorvald's dairyman.

When the world stopped spinning she skimmed her palms over the lad's body and soon understood his trouble. There was little her magic could do to help him, but she knew what would.

Several minutes later Aren and Benoia returned, having settled his horse for the night and gathered more wood.

"Do you know what ails the boy?" Aren asked.

"Vali's in Exhaustion."

Aren's brows rose. "Exhaustion? Does that still happen?"

"It does when a Talent Emerges late and the person isn't cared for properly. How old would you say he is? Fifteen summers?"

Aren tilted his head in thought, and then nodded. "That makes sense. When the trace we encountered faded and returned I thought we followed a weak or untrained Talent. Apparently his is just a very *new* Talent."

Annikke nodded her agreement.

"What can we do for him?" Benoia asked. "Exhaustion can kill, can't it?"

"It can." Annikke knew better than to hope that Aren had any *stirkedrikk* in his bags. He'd have had no reason to be packing the vilely sweet drink used for such a specific emergency. "We'll need to grind what food we have into a paste so we can get it down his throat as easily as possible. Other than that, all we can do is keep him warm."

She hoped it would be enough. Most such transitions, when a young person's Talent Emerged, took place at the onset of puberty. This young man was coming to it late, and apparently no one had cared enough for him to make sure he was safe and well fed to weather the demands on his body. Emergence Exhaustion was rare, but it could kill if a new Talent was overused.

Benoia and Annikke chopped their dried fruit and nuts into small pieces, crumbled some of Aren's journey-bread into the mix, making a gruel with water warmed by their small fire. They fed Vali like a baby bird every candlemark. He never opened his eyes, but he knew enough to swallow and open his mouth for more. The moon was high when Annikke finally persuaded Benoia to get some rest.

"Wake me when you tire and I'll spell you," Benoia said as she curled up in one of the two blankets they hadn't wrapped around the young man.

Annikke nodded. Doing what she was good at, caring for another, had eased some of the shadow in Benoia's eyes. Harming someone with her magic had shaken the girl, even if she'd done it to protect herself, even if she'd done it without meaning to. Annikke wasn't happy for Vali's condition, but she couldn't help but be glad his need had helped her foster-daughter forget what had happened to her, at least for a little while.

Aren sat a few feet away with his back to the fire, looking out into the forest, his bow unstrung but close at hand.

Benoia's breath quickly settled into the rhythm of sleep. Annikke pulled the remaining blanket around her shoulders and stared at her daughter's form, wrapped in flickering firelight. What would become of her? Calling on the Jarl for justice still seemed the best course, better than fleeing and always fearing pursuit. But what if Lord Dahleven found Benoia to be in the wrong? He might condemn her for the use of Elven magic alone. And her accuser was another lord. It wouldn't be the first time a powerful man had taken the side of another man of power.

"She's a good girl." Aren spoke softly, his deep voice a comforting rumble.

Why should she think the man's voice *comforting*? And yet it was.

"She is. Freya blessed me the day her father sold her into my care."

"The goddess blessed you both."

Annikke felt her color rise at the compliment, and was glad he gazed out at the dark forest instead of at her.

"She reminds me of my Tandra. Feisty and brave. They would like each other."

Annikke looked over at him. He was half turned away from her and light from their small fire danced over his broad shoulders. "How old is she, your daughter?"

"Fifteen summers. She came to me unlooked for, but she's been a delight every day of her life."

"Unlooked for?" Most parents knew well in advance that their family was growing.

Aren gazed into the forest and didn't speak for a moment, and Annikke wondered what tail she'd stepped on.

When he spoke, Aren's voice was flat. "Her mother didn't want the raising of her, and gave her into my keeping. I can only be grateful that she and her parents decided they didn't want my get until after the babe had quickened and ending her pregnancy would have been too dangerous."

His get. "You and Tandra's mother didn't part on good terms."

"We did not."

"You were both young."

"We were. But it wasn't my youth that her family objected to." His tone indicated that further questions wouldn't be welcome.

What a sad beginning to the girl's life. And yet, if Aren's warmth when he spoke her was any indication, Tandra was well loved, and likely knew no lack.

Vali stirred and licked his lips. Annikke spooned more of the paste into his mouth until he turned his head away.

"Why do you suppose he's out here on his own?"

"He's late coming into his Talent. Perhaps he despaired of being Talentless, and fled his home rather than be seen as less than a man."

Annikke nodded, and then realized Aren wouldn't see. "I can understand that. I thought many times of leaving my village when I was younger, but there was no fleeing my hair. All who see me know I'm Fey-marked."

"The smith spoke well of you. And others as well."

Annikke smiled. "The smith and his wife are good people. Better than most. It has taken half my life to gain some acceptance by the others though. Most people judge quickly and on appearance. I hope the Jarl is able to look deeper." She began chopping the rest of the fruit for another batch of gruel.

"Let me," Aren said, holding out his hand for the knife. "You should rest. I'll look after the boy."

For a moment Annikke thought to protest. She was the healer, after all, even if her particular gifts didn't extend to Emergence Exhaustion. Then common sense prevailed over her stubborn pride. The day had been a long one, beginning with the fear of capture by Lord Tholvar's men, a rush through the forest, and then riding a horse for the first time. Her body ached in ways she hadn't known possible. She handed him the knife handle first. "If he grows fevered or fails to take food, wake me."

Aren nodded. "Rest easy, mistress. I'll call you if there's need."

Annikke awoke as a dark dawn revealed skies that threatened rain. Although Aren had promised to wake Benoia for a turn at sitting with Vali, she saw that he'd let both of them rest. Annikke couldn't find the energy to take him to task for his sacrifice; her eyes still felt gritty from scant sleep and Benoia's face was more relaxed in slumber than Annikke had seen it since Sveyn had ruined their lives with his selfishness. Was it only five days ago? It seemed like half a lifetime.

When Annikke returned from seeing to her body's demands, Aren said softly, "We haven't enough food between us if he keeps eating like this. I'll have to hunt today."

"Fresh meat would be welcome."

"I don't welcome this delay, but—"

"We can't move him, given his condition," Annikke finished.

Aren's mouth curled at the corner, acknowledging their accord. Annikke couldn't help noticing that he had a fine mouth, with a full lower lip. He kept his beard trimmed short in the new fashion, and his dark hair braided back. A few wavy tendrils had worked themselves loose, and she wondered for just a moment what it would feel like to comb her fingers through his hair.

"Did someone say meat?"

Vali's question shattered her foolish thoughts. Annikke blushed, hoping Aren couldn't guess what she'd been thinking.

"A haunch of venison, or even a rabbit, would be welcome indeed." Vali's voice was unexpectedly deep given his lack of years, though weak.

"I did," Annikke said. "But we are, in fact, lacking the same. How are you feeling?"

"Like a mountain fell on me. What happened?"

"You fell over a cliff," Aren said. "And you're in Emergence."

Vali's expression of surprise would have been amusing if Annikke hadn't guessed how much it meant to the young man. In a tone that conveyed both his fear to hope and nascent elation, he asked, "Are you sure?"

Given his age, he and his parents, every person around him in fact, would have been wondering if he would take his full place in his family. Though it was rare for someone to not develop a Talent, those who didn't were seen as *less*. Even a useless Talent was better than none.

"We're sure," Aren answered. "We followed your path for much of the afternoon yesterday. Your tracks faded in an out."

"Oh. I was trying to do that. I'm pretty good at woodcraft." Vali's tone was equal parts disappointment and pride. "My uncle taught me."

"So am I, boy, as well as being a Tracker. Be assured, I wouldn't have lost your trail for a moment if your Talent hadn't obscured it part of the time."

Vali lifted himself on his elbows and searched Aren's face intently. "Are you sure?"

"I am. It's early days yet, but once you learn to use it, I expect your Talent will be a strong one."

Vali's eyes widened with hope and he released a deep breath. "I can go home."

"And where is home?" Annikke asked.

The young man's gaze slid away from hers. "Across the river."

Annikke glanced at Aren, who lifted a brow. He'd noted the youth's evasiveness, too.

"Forsvaremur?" Aren asked.

Vali nodded, his expression tight.

"How does your father serve Lady Solveig?"

Again Vali hesitated. "My father is dead. My uncle is a hunter. He's teaching me." He grimaced. "Though not well enough, if you found me. He taught me to track and to hide my own sign. I thought I'd done well, but it's hard to move at speed and be careful."

"Don't blame your teacher, Vali. You failed to change direction when you hid your trail."

Chagrin twisted the youth's expression. "My uncle will have my hide for that beginner's mistake."

"Be glad of your oversight this time. Had I not stumbled upon your trail I might not have found you, and Exhaustion would have taken you."

"I did so poorly?"

Aren gave young man half a smile. "No. Your uncle taught you well. It was probably just your Exhaustion that caused you to forget some of his lessons. I'm a Tracker Talent in service to Lord Dahleven."

Vali swallowed hard and looked away.

Why does that make the boy uncomfortable?

"Why did you leave?" Annikke asked when the silence had begun to stretch.

"Why do you think? I had no Talent."

"Mind your tone, boy," Aren growled.

Annikke turned a startled glance on Aren, then looked away. She wasn't used to people standing up for her.

Vali turned to Aren, mouth open to argue, but then the youth swallowed the retort that clearly had been on the tip of his tongue. When he spoke again it was in a milder voice. "I had no Talent, and I've a brother coming up behind me. I didn't want to burden my mother and uncle with the need to disinherit me."

Annikke's gaze sharpened. That probably meant Vali's father had left something worth inheriting. Some parents wouldn't have hesitated. Benoia's father for one. Others though, would find such a decision wrenching.

But a Talentless son couldn't inherit, no matter how much he was loved, and to be no better than a dependent for the rest of his life could sour a man. Many would have seen him as less than a cripple. Vali was well spoken. Minor nobility, perhaps? Or a well-to-do merchant's son? Oftentimes the less there was, the more precious it was held.

Aren nodded, apparently satisfied with this explanation.

"I hope you at least left a note," Benoia said, sitting up in her blankets and rubbing the sleep from her eyes. "If your mother is anything like Annikke, she'll have your skin for worrying her like this."

Vali's expression became sheepish.

Benoia snorted. "You didn't did you?"

"I did. I told them I was out hunting."

"That's even worse," Benoia said. "Now she thinks you could be lying in a ditch, eaten by wolves."

"I didn't want them looking for me too soon," Vali protested.

"Enough," Aren said. "What's done is done. First we need to fill your belly and get you strong enough to travel. Then you can return home to face your family. In the meantime, rest." He turned to Annikke. "I'll gather more wood, and then hunt us up something to eat."

Aren Tracked a small herd of deer to a pretty little glade which their spoor had shown him was a favorite grazing area, and settled in to wait. There was no point in chasing them through the forest when they'd likely be returning here before dusk.

As the shadows lengthened his mind kept churning. He imagined Benoia, frightened and angry, struggling to stop a spoiled lordling from taking her against her will, and more often than not Benoia's face became that of his daughter, Tandra. His stomach twisted. He was *glad* she'd stopped him, even if she'd used some kind of magic to do it. But would Lord Dahleven see it as he did? The Jarl had a daughter still in nappies, but he was also a leader who had to keep his lords' support. Would placating Lord Tholvar take precedence over justice?

Aren's hands tightened on his bow. Could he justify putting Benoia at risk? He owed a debt to Torlon, and he'd sworn not to bring grief to Annikke, or, by extension, Benoia. Yet he couldn't fail to escort her to Quartzholm. He'd also sworn to serve Lord Fender and through him, the Jarl.

Was this how his father had felt?

Aren had always regarded his father's action through a filter of anger and guilt. That anger was deserved. His father had failed to answer his lord's summons to a border skirmish, and with the lack of his leadership good men had died. It hadn't mattered that his father had remained at home to stay with his ailing wife. He'd broken his oath.

Had Aren not been out hunting and not expected back till the morrow, his father could have kept faith. But neither Aren nor his father had known the call would come that day.

Still, his father could have kept his promise. Their neighbor's wife would have stayed with Aren's mother if she'd only been asked, but a longstanding feud and his father's pride had prevented him from seeking aid from that quarter.

For the first time Aren wondered, what had his father felt when he decided to deny the oath he'd sworn? Knowing full well what the consequences would be, and that the taint of breaking faith with his lord would fall upon Aren and his mother, too, how had his father made that choice?

Aren refused to do that again to his mother, or to his daughter. Whatever the cost, Aren had to fulfill his duty to Lord Fender and the Jarl.

A flickering in the shadows drew his attention. A multi-pronged buck nosed out into the small clearing, seeking the scent of danger on the sweet summer air. Aren held still. Satisfied, the buck led his small family of two does, a tiny spotted fawn, and a half grown male into the open to graze the new green grass. Thanking the gods for their gift, Aren drew, aimed, and let fly.

chapter thirteen

ΛΝΝΙΚΚΕ WΛΤCHED VΛLI'S chest rise and fall gently in the deep slumber typical of young males. He'd fallen asleep again after eating a sizable quantity of Aren's journey-bread drizzled with the last of her honey.

He hasn't told us his full story.

Aren knew it, too, although he hadn't said any-thing. They'd merely exchanged a look and known they were in agreement. Neither of them considered whatev-er secrets the boy was keeping to be dangerous. Aren wouldn't have left Annikke and Benoia alone with him if he'd thought so. She had no way to know that about him, but she did.

Benoia lightly touched Vali's neck, seeking the pulse of his life. "He's much stronger now," she said softly.

Annikke nodded.

Benoia pulled her lower lip between her teeth.

Something was troubling the girl, which was hardly surprising given what she'd been through this last sevenday. Annikke rose and gestured for Benoia to follow her a little way apart from the youth so their conversation wouldn't wake him. Not that it was likely to, given how far he still had to go to recover.

"Tell me," Annikke said in her usual brisk way.

"I know Aren said the Jarl is a fair man, but can we really be sure? What promises has the Jarl made to Lord Tholvar that he must keep? He may only want Aren to find us so he can turn us over to Tholvar. We're only women, and men can do what they will with us."

With what Benoia had endured in her father's house and with Sveyn, Annikke couldn't fault the girl for her sour regard of men.

"I can't bear it that I've put you at risk," Benoia continued. "I ought to take this chance while Aren is gone to run as far from here as possible, but I've given my parole. It's me that he was sent to find and take to Quartzholm. I'll go. But there's no need for you to suffer because of what I did. You should return home to the cottage."

Annikke's heart twisted as Benoia made her selfless and foolish offer. "Silly girl, I've given Aren my parole as well. I can no more run off than you."

Benoia shook her head. "He'll release you from it. We both needn't go. I don't believe Aren will harm me, and Vali is on the mend. I can see to his health as well as the two of us together can."

If Benoia could see that Aren was an honorable man despite what Sveyn had tried to do, Annikke had hope that her girl could again find some happiness—if Lord Dahleven permitted.

And Aren *was* an honorable man. It made no sense, but Annikke trusted him even though she'd known him barely a day.

"You can, indeed, but you won't have to." Annikke's throat tightened as she pulled Benoia into a tight embrace. "I could never find any joy in our cottage, even if Lord Tholvar allowed me to, if I left you to face your fate alone. Whatever fate the Norns may weave—"

Stealthy movement in the forest froze the words on Annikke's tongue. Aren had left in another direction, and he wouldn't be sneaking back into camp. Quickly she returned to Vali's side and slipped the dagger he'd carried from its sheath. Benoia hefted a branch from the firewood as a club.

It wasn't an animal that kept coming closer, striding between the tree trunks. It was a man carrying a long knife.

His face broke into a grin as he saw them. "Len! Boyart! Morlegg! I've found them," he shouted over his shoulder.

From the dappled forest shadows a voice called, "What? I can't hear you, I'm taking a piss."

The man lifted his gaze to the sky as if asking Odin for patience, then looked back to Annikke and Benoia. His grin faded as he took in Vali's still form. "Did you maim him with your dark magic, too?"

"Leave here." Annikke tried to make her voice firm. "Or I'll do the same to you."

She felt Benoia's surprise at her threat though she didn't dare spare her foster-daughter a glance.

"I don't think so, mistress." A man's voice came from Annikke's right and she heard the creak of a bow being drawn. "You'll not get close enough to cast your spells."

"A timely arrival, Len," the first man said. "Now put down your weapons. I'll not tell you twice."

Benoia threw her branch away. "It's me you want. Leave Annikke out of it." She stepped forward.

"No!" Annikke jerked Benoia back behind her. In that short time the first man had covered half the distance to them. Annikke thrust the knife in her hand outward. "Stay back!"

"What's going on?" Vali struggled to sit up. He blinked away sleep, then his expression became fierce as he took in the drawn weapons and the tension. "Forest bandits," he sneered. "Be gone! There's nothing for you here." His tone belonged to someone who was used to being obeyed.

"Well aren't you the little lordling!" The man with the knife laughed, barely sparing a glance for Vali as he advanced on Annikke. "You should learn to mind your tongue, boy."

The next thing she knew, he'd knocked both Annikke and her blade to the ground.

"Leave her alone!" Benoia lunged to push the man back, but he just backhanded her aside.

He knelt and pressed his knife against Annikke's throat. "Back off, witch, or I'll cut her!"

The steel was cold and sharp on her skin. Annikke didn't dare move.

Benoia froze, still as ice where she'd fallen. "Don't!"

"Len, tie her up." The man jerked his head at Benoia.

"I'm not touching her."

"I'll do it," a third male voice said. "I'm not afraid of a girl. A pretty one, at that. We could have some fun here, before we take them back."

Horror made Annikke jump and distant pain sliced her neck. "Don't you touch her!" She wouldn't let another animal threaten her daughter that way. Not again. Her captor pushed her down with a hard hand between her breasts.

"Don't you know what she did, Boyart?" Len asked. "Shriveled Lord Sveyn's cock so it looks like a root left too long in the cellar. My Helga saw it when the Healer came. He couldn't do nothing for it, neither. I'm not getting my dick anywhere near her."

Boyart laughed as he tied Benoia hand and foot. "Well, if my dick was starting out as small as yours I'd be worried, too. Lucky for me, I got a whole lot more to share."

Vali lunged to his feet, a burning brand in both hands. "Let them go!" he commanded in a voice that was stronger than his legs.

"Put it down boy," yet another voice said from beyond Annikke's field of vision.

How many of them are there?

Vali swung around, brandishing the flaming branch. There was the sound of wood hitting wood once, twice. Vali grunted with effort, and then a new man advanced and pushed the now disarmed youth back down onto his blankets. Vali gathered himself to rise again.

The man pointed his staff at him. "Don't be stupid, boy. Give me your parole, or I'll truss you up like these witches and leave you to rot in the forest." He nodded at Annikke and Benoia.

"Do as he says," Annikke said.

"Listen to her. We have no quarrel with you."

Vali's face twisted with anger. "I won't give my parole to a coward who threatens women."

The man standing over Vali lifted his hand and there was the sound of a slap. "When you're out of leading strings you can talk to me of cowardice, boy. Until then, keep your mouth shut." The man drew a leather thong from his belt and knotted Vali's wrists together.

"You've no right to—" Vali protested.

"That's where you're wrong. We're here on Lord Sveyn's business."

"Be quiet, Morlegg!" the man with the knife commanded.

"You lie," Vali said. "You wear no lord's sigil."

Morlegg cuffed Vali on the back of the head this time. "Mind your manners, pup! Or I'll gag you, too."

Annikke jerked, wanting to intervene, but the thirsty blade bit her neck.

"Perhaps you should learn to mind yours." A woman dressed in green and brown leathers stood at the forest's edge. She was perhaps ten years older than Annikke, with brown hair tightly clubbed at the base of her neck. Her drawn bow was steady and aimed squarely between Morlegg's shoulder blades.

Morlegg whipped around as the woman spoke, then froze as he saw the archer intently aiming at his chest.

Off to the side, Len shifted his aim to the new threat.

"Draw down." Another woman spoke from just behind Len. "My blade is hungry for a foolish man's blood."

Len squawked, and Annikke spared him a glance. Standing behind him, a plump woman a few summers senior to Benoia had her dagger pressed against his throat. Annikke had been so focused on Morlegg and Vali she hadn't seen or heard the women approach. Apparently, neither had Len. He let his string go slack and unnocked his arrow.

"Drop it," she commanded. "The bow, too."

"This is no concern of yours," the man pressing the knife to Annikke's throat interrupted. It bit deeper and she felt a drop of blood tickle down her neck. "These women are wanted by Lord Tholvar. They used Odin's dark *seidhr* to maim his son. You're interfering with the Jarl's justice."

"Drop your weapons," the first woman ordered. "Then you can complain all you want." When he hesitated, she added, "Or I can let fly my arrow and you'll be short a friend. I'll not miss at this range. You choose."

"Stevek?" Morlegg said, lifting his hands. "I'm not interested in dying for this."

"They're just women," Boyart sneered from where he still knelt beside Benoia. He had a knife in his hand pressed hard against Benoia's belly. "They don't have the balls to kill. But I do. And if you don't back off, I'll slice this witch open so Fenrir can eat her guts. Now *you* put down your weapons."

"And spread our legs so you can show us what we've been missing?" The woman aiming at Morlegg asked.

Boyart leered. A second later an arrow from an unseen archer sprouted from his eye.

Stevek tossed his knife aside.

Annikke jumped to her feet and ran to Benoia. Using Boyart's blade, she cut her daughter's bonds and gathered her close. "Are you all right?"

"Are *you*?" Benoia touched the bloody cut on Annikke's neck.

Annikke felt warmth as Benoia's touch healed her and the sting faded. "Don't," she murmured. "Not now."

Her foster-daughter looked stricken. "I didn't mean to," she breathed.

"Now drop your arrow and bow!" The plump woman prodded Len with her knife.

Instead Len stabbed backward with the arrow in his fist. The woman yelped, but as Len spun, swinging his bow like a club, she danced aside. Quicker than Annikke could see, she stabbed him in the back below his ribs. With an agonized scream the man's back arched and he fell. A moment later he lay still, blood staining the ground beneath his body.

Stevek turned and charged, bellowing with rage, another knife appearing in his hand. An instant later an arrow sprouted from his shoulder, another from his neck. He staggered, hands clutching at his throat. His momentum carried him forward to his target, but the woman stepped aside as he toppled at her feet.

Morlegg ran for the trees. A third woman emerged from the forest on Annikke's left, an arrow on the string. She drew and loosed, but the arrow thunked into a tree as the man fled into the forest. She started to sprint after him, but the first woman called out, "Let him go."

Annikke watched, dumb and still. She'd never seen such a thing. She'd heard tales of shield maidens from ages past, but she'd never imagined meeting women who could fight like Valkyries and win against armed men.

"Were there only the four of them?" the first woman asked, drawing Annikke's attention.

Benoia answered. "They're all we saw."

The woman nodded, and spoke to the other two women. "Kalin, scout the area."

Kalin acknowledged the order with a tip of her blond head, then disappeared back beneath the trees.

"I'm Norva," the first woman introduced herself, "and that's Halageth." She indicated the plump woman.

Annikke noted that the woman didn't use their patronyms in her introduction. Were they Outcasts? Even if they were, they'd just saved Benoia from being abducted by Lord Tholvar's men. For that alone, she owed them courtesy, even if their actions were likely to make a bad situation worse. Lord Tholvar would no doubt blame Benoia for the death of his men. "I'm Annikke Torrsonsdatter, and this is my foster-daughter, Benoia Fornosdatter. I thank you for your timely arrival and intervention."

Norva nodded. "Merely repaying a debt, since you found and cared for Lord Vali."

Annikke lifted a brow and looked down at the youth in his blankets. "*Lord* Vali?"

"Aye," Hallageth said as she rose from cutting the young man free of his bonds. "This is Lady Solveig's son, and heir to Forsvaremur. Did you not know?"

A slew of questions crowded Annikke's tongue, but she kept her answer short. "No. He didn't choose to confide that to us."

"I renounced my inheritance. I'm not a lord anymore." Vali, *Lord* Vali, struggled to his feet.

It was Norva's turn to look surprised. "You did *what*? Are you daft, boy? I mean, my lord." In a voice half directed at herself, she said, "Lady Solveig's messenger said nothing of this." She waved her hand. "Never mind. That's between you and your lady mother. All I know, all I care about, is returning you to her."

Vali drew himself up. "I'm not a lost puppy."

"Could have fooled me," Hallageth muttered.

Norva shot her companion a quelling glance. "Nevertheless, my lord, Lady Solveig has tasked everyone able to leave their duties with finding you, even the Daughters of Freya."

Halageth steadied him as Vali wobbled.

Norva looked alarmed. "Are you unwell, my lord?" She speared Annikke with a fear sharpened gaze. "What's wrong with him?"

"Emergence Exhaustion. You wouldn't happen to have any *stirkedrikk*, would you?"

"Baldur's bright shiny ... buttons," Norva swore. "What were you thinking, to leave when you were in Emergence? My lord."

"I wasn't *in* Emergence when I left."

Vali began to shake, and Benoia moved to bracket him with Halageth on his other side.

"You'd best sit down before you fall down," Benoia said, helping him back to his nest of blankets.

"Damn," Norva swore, "I don't have any *stirkedrikk*."

"Yes, we do," Halageth said.

Norva looked at her companion, brows raised.

Hallageth shrugged, her expression sheepish. "The

messenger said to bring some, just in case. I threw a flask in my pack and forgot about it." She left to retrieve her sack from the forest. A few minutes later Annikke had administered the extremely sweet draught while Vali made a disgusted face.

"Bleh. That's vile," he complained.

"Will that be enough?" Norva asked.

"I don't know. Aren is out hunting. It will be a while before he returns, but until then we've got journey-bread." Annikke matched words to action, handing a piece to the young lord.

Vali made a face but took the dry round and bit into it with a crunch.

"Here." Halageth dug into her pack and produced a wooden cup into which she poured an amber liquid. "Soak it in this cider so you don't break a tooth."

"My thanks." Vali accepted the cup and fell upon the journey-bread with a ferocity only seen in starving wolves and youths in Emergence.

The women watched in silence with a kind of awe that he could still be that hungry even after drinking the *stirkedrikk*. Vali had barely finished and set down the empty cup when his eyes drooped.

Annikke knelt to pull the blanket close around his sleeping form.

Norva squatted on lean haunches on the other side of Vali. "Is that normal?" She didn't try to keep the worry out of her voice. "I've never seen Emergence take someone like this before."

"Nor have I," Annikke answered. "But he is late coming to it, and he'd used his Talent unknowing for days before we found him. Had Aren not been able to track him..."

"We think that he'll be all right as long as we keep him fed and let him rest," Benoia added.

"Thank the gods. The Daughters of Freya owe Lady

Solveig much. I wouldn't want us to be the bearers of tragic news."

"I think instead that you'll be bringing her the happy tidings that not only is her son restored to her, but he is fully a man with a powerful Talent, and able to inherit his place as Jarl."

Kalin emerged silently from between two trees and answered Norva's unspoken query. "No sign of others, except for one set of tracks that are candlemarks older than theirs." She tilted her head at the men lying on the ground. "The tracks lead off yonder and don't intersect with the way these four approached." She pointed back the way she'd come, in the same place Aren had disappeared into the dappled green.

"Those would be Aren's tracks," Annikke said. "He's hunting, since we've fed most of our food to Vali."

Halageth rose to pace the perimeter of the small clearing and Kalin took her place watching the forest over Norva's shoulder.

"If it's not a secret, will you tell me about the Daughters of Freya?" Benoia asked.

"It's not a secret," Norva answered. "We are wives and mothers and daughters who couldn't find justice from the men who had power over us. We had nowhere to run to until Lady Solveig gave us the use of fallow land."

"That's why you don't use your patronyms?" Annikke asked.

"We see no reason to use the names of men who beat us, or used us against our will, or sold us into thralldom to pay their debts. At home we call ourselves by our mother's name. There I'm known as Norva Maeligsdatter."

"I like that. That's how I'd like to be known. Benoia Annikkesdatter."

"You have a mother," Annikke said softly.

"I do, but she never stood up for me. She let Da beat her, and me. I'd rather be known by your name." Her fierce expression suddenly turned doubtful. "Is that all right?"

Annikke blinked, willing her tears away. "Of course."

Benoia nodded as if it was all settled. "Do all of the Daughters of Freya know how to fight the way you did?"

"Most of us. Sometimes an angry father or husband comes looking to reclaim the woman he drove away. We learn how to protect ourselves."

"I'd like that," Benoia said. "What do I have to do to join you?"

"Benoia," Annikke protested. "You don't know these women."

"I know I don't ever want a man to touch me the way Sveyn did. I don't ever want to be afraid like that again. And what if my father stops selling me to you? What if you can't pay? Should I let him sell me to someone else, or let him beat and starve me again?"

Annikke twisted her hands together. She and Benoia hadn't talked much about what her life had been like under her father's roof. Annikke had just been fiercely glad to trade her healing potions and hangover remedies to keep Benoia away from Fornos.

The look Norva slid between Annikke and her foster-daughter held shrewd understanding of the loss Annikke feared. "You would be welcome as well," she said.

"Even Fey-marked as I am? Are the Daughters of Freya so welcoming?"

Norva remained silent and looked away. Annikke shook her head. "I thought not."

The older woman stood. "We have housekeeping to do. Let's get these bodies out of camp."

Norva and Benoia moved the bodies of Morlegg's

companions away from their camp. Annikke cleaned and bound the stab wound Len had inflicted that Halageth finally admitted was paining her, and used a touch of her magic to keep the shallow puncture from festering. Halageth raised her eyebrows at the sensation, but said nothing beyond offering her thanks.

The three Daughters of Freya traded the duty of patrolling the forest around their little camp twice. Annikke fed Vali again, and again he fell asleep as soon as he'd eaten. Kalin taught Benoia how to break the grasp of a man by unexpectedly moving closer, and to not run until her opponent was down and disabled. Annikke's heart ached as she watched Benoia's brows draw together in concentration as she knocked the plump woman on her arse and faked a blow to her groin.

Kalin laughed. "Well done! You're a quick learner."

Benoia grinned as she clasped the other woman's arm to help her up. "I wish I'd known how to do this a sevenday ago."

Annikke wished that, too, but even if Benoia had defended herself without magic, they'd probably have needed to flee anyway. Sveyn would still have sought revenge for his bruised pride.

Kalin smiled sadly. "None can unravel what the Norns have woven. At least you know it now."

A nightingale trilled in the woods, and Kalin's posture sharpened. She drew her knife. "Someone's coming." Then she faded into the trees.

Aren pulled up short some distance from where he'd left Annikke and Benoia to survey the ground, the foliage, and the trees. The signs were subtle, but they were there for any good hunter to find, let alone one with a Tracker

Talent. Multiple people had passed by here, and none of the tracks belonged to Annikke or Benoia.

Using all his woodcraft, Aren silently backed away a good distance, cached the young buck he'd shot and cleaned, then nocked an arrow. Spiraling around the clearing, he watched for watchers and listened for careless conversation, or, gods forbid, cries of distress.

He hadn't gone far before he found the bodies of three men lying side by side. A spike of alarm jolted his heart. It was too much to hope that this violence hadn't touched Annikke and Benoia, but at least it wasn't their bodies lying here. Aren pushed down the impulse to rush into their camp to reassure himself that they were all right, and looked closer at the dead. The bodies were marred by arrow and stab wounds. Annikke and Benoia hadn't killed these men. Others had done so, and it was far more likely to be the result of a falling out amongst Outcasts than it was to have been honorable men defeating ruffians. Even if there'd been a battle between good men and evil, these fallen could be the good.

Instead of following his desire, he continued on his inward circle until he found a place where repeated tracks indicated a path that had been traveled more than once by a perimeter guard. He obscured any trace of his own passage, then tucked himself back among the undergrowth and settled in for his second hunt of the day.

He hadn't long to wait.

The sun had moved less than a handspan when Aren heard someone coming. A few moments later a tall, well-rounded woman passed by his hiding spot carrying a bow. She moved carefully, making little noise. Aren held still. The woman paused as she crossed the place where he'd stopped to read tracks, casting her gaze about as she examined the ground for sign. Aren held his breath. If the woman had a Talent for Tracking equal or better than his own, she'd see through his tricks.

He waited, watching as she searched the area. When the woman finally moved on, Aren released a pent up breath.

The next person to pass by his hiding place was a slender woman who was as silent as the breeze. She didn't hesitate as she passed by.

Aren continued to wait. He'd seen seven different sets of tracks as he'd circled the clearing. He could assume that three of them belonged to the dead men. That left four.

The third woman didn't follow the same route as the other two. She traveled a wider path, passing beyond Aren, but still not seeing him in his hide. When the first woman again passed by at the expected interval, Aren had seen enough. Only three women were patrolling the camp. He guessed these were Daughters of Freya, though why they were *here*, he couldn't guess, unless it had something to do with Vali. That left one set of tracks unaccounted for. The others he'd seen were large and had to belong to men, and three of them were dead.

It was time to sort out this mystery.

Aren had heard the usual rumors about Freya's Daughters, but since they apparently had defeated at least three men he wasn't going to underestimate them just because they were women. The odds were at least three to one against him, and they'd already proven their willingness to kill. He didn't think they would harm Annikke and Benoia, but there was only one way to find out if he'd already failed to repay his debt to the Elves. He stood up, returned his arrow to its quiver, and then made his way noisily toward the camp.

chapter fourteen

"ᴀʀᴇɴ!" Annikke stood when she saw him, a smile lighting her face.

Safe. Annikke and Benoia, sitting near Vali, were both safe. Aren released a breath he hadn't known he was holding.

A second later the force of Annikke's smile struck him. It transformed her, and for an instant all other thought left Aren's mind. She was lovely without her perpetually worried expression, and he found himself smiling back as if they were the only ones in the clearing.

Her smile faded. "No luck?"

Aren dragged his attention back to where it needed to be. A quick scan showed no strangers in their camp.

"Where are our guests?" Aren held his bow loosely in one hand at his side, and his other well away from his dagger. He didn't want to die from a misunderstanding.

"Here," a feminine voice answered. The smallest of the three women he'd seen emerged from the trees beyond his left shoulder, a drawn bow in her hands.

Aren turned slightly to better see her. She held her bow steady and sure, and he had no doubt she'd loose at the least threat. And there were the other two, still out of sight.

"Norva, this is Aren. He's ... escorting us to Quartzholm," Annikke said.

"He's taking me there to answer for the crime of defending myself," Benoia added.

"Do you work for the same Lord Tholvar that those others claimed to serve?"

"No."

"Benoia?" Norva asked as she continued to gaze at Aren down the length of her arrow.

"I don't think so," Benoia admitted. "He said he serves the Jarl."

"He's not a threat," Annikke said to Norva. "Not like those others. You can draw down."

Norva relaxed her string, but kept her arrow nocked. Aren turned his attention to Annikke, grateful that she thought at least that much of him. "What happened?"

"Some men came into the camp and said they were going to take us to Lord Tholvar. Or maybe Sveyn. One said they served the Jarl. They were a little confused on the subject. They got violent when Norva and her friends arrived and started asking questions."

Something twisted in Aren's gut, something more than the shame that he'd failed in his duty. "Did they hurt you?"

A shadow passed over her face. Something had happened, but she said, "No, thanks to these Daughters of Freya."

Aren closed his eyes, as a storm surge of relief flooded him. He didn't want to think about how Annikke and Benoia might have fared in the care of Tholvar's men. His throat was unexpectedly tight as he spoke. "My thanks, Norva."

"We saw a woman at knife's point. That doesn't sit well with us."

"I'm in your debt." His debts would soon bury him, but this was one he'd gladly pay.

Norva shook her head. "Nay. You saved the heir to Forsvaremur. We're even."

Aren cast a look at Vali's slumbering form. "Lady Solveig's son, eh?" He turned back to Norva. "Since neither of us want to bring harm to Annikke, Benoia, or Vali, perhaps your two companions could stop aiming their arrows at me?"

Norva lifted a brow, and then trilled a whistle like a whippoorwill's call. "They will continue to keep watch, however."

The feeling in Aren's back that felt like target had been tacked there eased. He gave her half a smile. "It's only prudent."

The wiry woman advanced closer, looking at the youth curled in his blankets. "How long before Lord Vali can travel?"

Annikke shrugged. "His body will tell us. It would have been better if your hunt had been successful," she added to Aren. "He needs more food than we have."

"Did you think I'd come into an armed camp hampered with a carcass? Build up the fire, we're eating venison tonight."

Annikke leaned forward, legs crossed tailor fashion, a warm cup of tea in her hands. Her belly was full, Vali had some color in his face again, and in company with Aren and the Daughters of Freya, her fear of Lord Tholvar's men was in abeyance. Trouble still stalked her and Benoia, but for the first time in a week, worry wasn't in the forefront of her mind.

Dusk gave way to night. Norva had just returned from her sweep of the perimeter, and Kalin had slipped away for her patrol when Benoia said, "I want to go with Norva and the others when they take Vali home to Forsvaremur."

Annikke's fragile peace shattered at the thought of losing Benoia. But it wouldn't happen, not yet anyway. "You made a promise to Aren." She didn't look at him, but she felt Aren hold himself still, saying nothing.

"I promised to do him no harm, and to not try to escape. I haven't." She looked at Aren. "But if you let me go, that wouldn't be escaping."

"Benoia!" Annikke spoke sharply. "You can't ask a man to break his oath! Especially not so that you won't have to."

Her foster-daughter's expression grew both stricken and panicked. "I'm sorry! But what am I to do? We don't know who sent those men. Maybe the Jarl decided not to wait for Aren to bring me in. I'm just a poor girl from a small village. Maybe he just wants to make me go away."

Annikke shook her head. "Far more likely it was Sveyn who sent those men. Lord Fender said to come to him if we were ever in need. You trust *him* don't you? Would he serve an unworthy man?"

"Do lords keep their promises any better than other men?" Benoia asked bitterly.

Annikke cast an anxious glance at Aren at the implied insult. Even Norva's brows rose, but Aren remained silent, his expression drawn. Annikke held her breath. Any second now he'd put Benoia in her place. He might even decide that he couldn't trust her to keep her word and demand she submit to restraints. Would the

Daughters of Freya allow that? Would they come to blows?

"I promised to protect you, and I failed to do that," Aren said in a tightly controlled voice. "It's only by a gift of the gods, and the skill of the Daughters of Freya, that you weren't harmed. I am forsworn. But I will *not* fail to keep my oath to the Jarl. I *will* take you to Quartzholm."

Who was his promise to protect us given to then, if not the Jarl? Lord Fender?

"Moreover, I believe the only way to keep you both safe is to go to Quartzholm. Running to Forsvaremur isn't the answer."

"Sometimes running from danger is all a woman can do," Halageth said into the silence that followed his words.

"Sometimes, but not *this* time," Aren said. "Those men were *not* sent by the Jarl. I'd stake my life on it. I haven't been in Quartzholm long enough to know all by sight, but I do know what kind of man Lord Fender accepts into his service, and by extension, the Jarl. Those men would not behave as you've told me these did, nor were they wearing anything that identified them as being in the Jarl's service."

"That's all well and good, but what if the Jarl decides he needs to placate Lord Tholvar more than he cares about justice?" Benoia said. "Let me disappear among the Daughters of Freya."

Norva shook her head. "I cannot speak for Lord Dahleven, but what I do is on my head. I owe the Daughters of Freya too much to repay them by bringing the ire of Lord Dahleven to Lady Solveig's door. You could run to the Daughters of Freya, but we can't keep you from your Jarl if he commands your presence. We won't. We owe Lady Solveig too much."

Her foster-daughter pressed her lips together tightly and stared off into the distance. Annikke recognized the look as the one the girl wore when she wanted to argue but recognized it would do her no good. It didn't mean she'd given up, however.

"Even if Freya's Daughters would have you, it wouldn't be safe to go there now," Aren said.

Benoia looked at him with a sullen gaze, but Annikke could see he'd piqued her curiosity.

"The man who escaped? He surely recognized these women as Daughters of Freya. What other women could have fought so well? There's only one ferry crossing within a week's travel. Morlegg and his friends will be waiting for you there. But they have no reason to think you'll go to the Jarl. They won't look for you on the road to Quartzholm."

Benoia looked away again, and Annikke's heart broke to see a tear roll down her foster-daughter's cheek.

"Benoia," Aren said gently. He waited until she looked at him, then said, "I know you have little reason to trust men, but we are not all like your father or Sveyn. Lord Dahleven has a baby daughter. I do not believe he'll be able to hear your story without thinking of what justice he'd want for her."

"I hope you're right."

chapter fifteen

BIRDSONG BEGAN WITH the first greying of the sky, waking Aren as the day dawned bright and clear. Lady Solveig's son awoke looking better than he had since Aren had first seen him. As they broke their fast, Vali declared himself fit for travel and Annikke agreed, provided he rest and eat often.

"I'll see that he doesn't overtax himself," Norva promised.

The young lord rolled his eyes as he grinned. "You won't have to, Norva. Mistress Annikke will watch me with Heimdal's eye."

Norva frowned. "They're off to Quartzholm, my lord. We go to relieve Lady Solveig's worry in Forsvaremur."

Vali shook his head. "Send Kalin and Halageth with that message. I need to speak with Lord Dahleven on behalf of Benoia and Mistress Annikke. If not for their aid and Aren's, I'd be dead. They helped me not knowing who I was. I owe them."

Benoia's eyes widened. "Thank you."

"Aye, my lord. Quartzholm it is, then." Norva didn't look displeased.

Aren nodded. Vali was going to be a fine Jarl when his mother handed over Forsvaremur to him. "Quartzholm is the better choice for you both as well. You made no friend of Morlegg. You won't surprise him again, and if he is waiting at the ferry, he'll have more men with him. You'd all be better to return home with a larger escort."

"Aye," Kalin said, "but Halageth and I will chance the ferry crossing. My Talent will let me reconnoiter the landing without being noticed, and Lady Solveig should have word her son is safe sooner rather than later."

Aren couldn't fault that thinking, and the two women soon departed. His own party took a little longer to sort out. Vali tried to refuse when Aren said he should ride Pinter, wanting to let Annikke and Benoia ride. Aren respected him for it, but before he could disagree, Annikke pierced Vali with a look perfected by mother-hood. "You're still under my care, young lord, and *I* say you ride. If you walk, you'll need to rest every quarter candlemark. We'd best get to Quartzholm before Lord Dahleven grows impatient."

Lady Solveig's son had the grace to look sheepish, and climbed into the saddle. "You see Norva? Mistress Annikke will keep me in line."

The five of them made slow progress, partly because Aren called frequent rests. He said it was for the sake of the horse, but he wasn't going to let Vali tire himself. Besides the young lord, it was for Annikke's sake as well. Fatigue shadowed her eyes. She'd been sleeping on the hard ground for more than a week, eating meager rations. Whatever she'd done to mend Vali's arm, an arm Aren would have sworn was broken but that the boy now used freely, had taken even more out of her, and then she'd endured a violent assault. She needed rest almost as much as Vali, and if he'd had a second horse he would have made her ride.

Pines began to dominate as the elevation rose. The early summer undergrowth was minimal, but under the cover of fallen needles the ground was rocky and uneven. Aren chose a route through the forest that would intersect the road. "It's longer in distance, but ultimately shorter in time," he explained when Norva asked.

They made camp under the spreading boughs of an old, lone oak, sharing a meal of journey-bread, cider, and roasted venison as the light faded. Vali again ate like a starving wolf, but Benoia sat rigidly, wrapped tightly in a blanket even though the night hadn't yet grown cool, barely nibbling her ration. They would reach Quartzholm tomorrow, and no doubt the girl was nervous. Aren tried to think of some way to allay her fears, but he'd already said all he could. Her fate was in Lord Dahleven's hands.

"Sing us a song, Benoia," Annikke asked.

Benoia jumped, startled out of whatever thoughts were furrowing her brow. "I don't feel much like singing."

"Oh, yes! Please do," Vali said. "The Long Hunt! Do you know that one?"

Benoia chuckled, as Vali no doubt intended. He'd named a song sung at every festival.

"Of course."

Annikke nodded. "Good choice."

Aren could see Annikke was keeping her anxiety under tight rein, but even in the fading light he noticed how her knuckles whitened as she clasped her hands together tightly. Then Benoia began to sing, and the tension in her shoulders eased. Soon she was nodding her head in time with the song.

The young woman's voice was clear and sweet, and

she sang the nearly endless ballad about the adventures of a band of men hunting in an endless wood well, omitting the more ribald stanzas. Aren wondered if she knew them.

Probably, he thought. *The young always manage to learn such things. I wonder if Tandra knows those verses.*

Aren decided he didn't want to know, and joined Vali and Norva on the upbeat chorus. Was it Aren's imagination, or were the leaves swaying in time with the tune despite the lack of a breeze?

"Now you," Benoia commanded Annikke.

"You know better than to ask me to sing," Annikke protested.

Benoia laughed. "True enough. But you can tell us the story of the boys sheltered by the trees."

"That's a children's tale," Annikke protested.

"But a good one," Aren said. "And appropriate to the setting."

Annikke glanced up into the shadowed boughs spreading overhead and snorted delicately. "Very well."

It was too dark for Aren to see her face clearly, but Annikke's silver hair gleamed in the little light that remained. He imagined her smile twisting the corner of her mouth up with wry amusement.

"Long ago, there was a wood gatherer who lived on the edge of a vast forest with his two small children, Honeg and Gretna. He was a good man, but poor..."

The moon, just past full, was high in the sky when Aren returned from his turn at sentry duty. Annikke stood a short distance from camp, gazing into the shadowed forest, her arms wrapped tightly around her waist.

Moonlight reflected off her silver hair, making it look like molten metal. He'd never seen an Elf maiden, but he couldn't imagine they'd be any more beautiful. He paused just long enough to rouse Norva for her duty, and then gathered up one of his blankets.

Annikke didn't move as he approached, but as he laid the blanket over her shoulders, she said, "It was on a night such as this that they took me."

He hadn't thought she would speak of her experience with the Elves. He certainly wouldn't have asked, even though he'd wondered.

"For many years Midsummer's eve was a time of terror for me," she said in a voice as soft as a dove's call. "I didn't remember what had happened, and they kept coming back, year after year, knocking and knocking. I thought I would go mad. And then, when I couldn't endure it anymore, I opened the door and learned that my fear had all been for naught. I hope my fear for Benoia proves as unfounded."

"I do, too."

Annikke turned to him. The moonlight robbed her face of color. "I believe you. What you said about Lord Dahleven having a daughter, and wanting justice for her. You were really speaking for yourself, weren't you?"

Aren nodded. There was no point in denying it. "I'm doing this for her, for Tandra."

"How does taking Benoia in to face Lord Tholvar's justice benefit your daughter?"

"It won't be Lord Tholvar she faces, it will be Lord Dahleven."

"Since I don't know the Jarl or his motives, that's not much comfort," Annikke said. "You didn't answer my question."

He hadn't whispered secrets in the dark to a woman since before Tandra's birth, and those youthful secrets now paled in comparison. Annikke stood still and patient, waiting for his answer. The quiet night invited him to confide in her. "Bringing Benoia to Quartzholm, to the Jarl, is just one small step in my quest to restore honor to my family name."

"And?" Annikke asked when his pause lengthened. "What damaged your family's honor?"

Aren took a deep breath. Her good opinion shouldn't matter to him. It *didn't* matter, with respect to what he must do. He had a duty to perform. But some foolish part of him hoped she wouldn't think less of him, once she knew the truth. "My father is an Oathbreaker. *Was* an Oathbreaker. He couldn't face his shame, so first he left, and then he killed himself, leaving my mother and me, and ultimately Tandra, to face it for him."

He told her the whole story then, how he'd been out hunting overnight when his mother fell ill, as she often did. It was pure bad luck that Lord Fellig, the new lord of the province, called all men sworn to him to raid against a neighboring province. Aren's father, Birgir, had faithfully served Lord Fellig's father as an armsmaster, and had been given his own land as a reward. But he'd also promised the old lord that he'd serve his son, too, if called, and so he'd sworn fealty to Lord Fellig.

When the summons came, his father hadn't answered. He'd stayed by his wife's sickbed. They'd had a maidservant he could have entrusted her care to. He might have called upon the neighbor's wife, except that the men were at odds with one another over property and water, and his father was too proud to humble himself.

Even then, his father's faithlessness might have been forgiven, except that Lord Fellig was a poor leader of men. His raid had been soundly repulsed and several of his warriors had died. Fellig took back the land his father had given Birgir to pay *weregild* to the families of the dead men, and named Birgir Oathbreaker.

"And so we moved to an abandoned cottage on the edge of our village, and I kept my mother and myself fed by hunting, and clothed by selling furs. Trade was always at a steep price because I was my father's get, an Oathbreaker's son, and no one trusted me to make an honest bargain."

"And Tandra's mother repudiated you."

"Yes—" Aren coughed, his throat unexpectedly tight.

"Did you love her?"

Had he? Her rejection had been painful enough. "We were young and wanted each other. It might have grown into love if my father hadn't shamed us."

A moment later she put it all together. "And now Tandra is coming of age and you must salvage your family honor for the sake of her future."

"Yes."

Annikke was silent for what seemed to be a long time. In the distance a mockingbird trilled, pouring its heart into one song after another, apparently unaware or uncaring that it was the middle of the night and not time for such expressions. Aren grimaced, feeling as foolish as the bird. What madness had taken him, to make him reveal his family's shame to her? Was she appalled that she'd put her trust in him? Was she thinking that a promise given to an Oathbreaker's son wasn't binding?

"Your father must have loved your mother very much."

"*Love?*" Aren's voice was rough with incredulity. "If he loved her, if he cared for either of us, how could he saddle us with his dishonor?"

"If Tandra were gravely ill," she countered, "could you leave her?"

"Of course, if my duty demanded it. My mother

would look after her."

Annikke just stood there, arms crossed, holding the blanket tight around her, with one eyebrow raised in challenge, and he knew he'd just told a lie.

"No. I couldn't leave her." The horror of that threatened to choke him. He was no better than his father.

He turned without saying another word, and walked away.

Annikke walked silently beside Benoia, lost in her thoughts. Vali rode behind, with Norva bringing up the rear.

Aren had said very little to her, to anyone, this morning. Perhaps she shouldn't have said what she did the night before. Men needed their delusions. But Aren's had seemed to be hurting him, and she hated seeing him suffer. Now she'd just made whatever burden he carried heavier. He insisted on carrying it alone, and so he'd ranged ahead, returning only long enough to let Norva know that all was clear.

Apparently he regretted what he'd said the previous night and was trying to make up for it by uttering as little as possible to her now.

And who am I to say he should do differently?

It wasn't as if she often shared her concerns with others. The problem was, his story had touched her. Though her parents had barely been able to look at her after she'd been Fey-marked, they hadn't turned their backs on her. They'd even tried to protect her, as best they could. Aren, on the other hand, felt his da's choice as a personal betrayal. A rejection that diminished him.

He probably wished he hadn't shared his story with

her last night. But did he have to take his unhappiness out on all of them?

The ground had stopped rising by mid-morning. Now at mid-day they were descending again into woods dominated by trees that dropped their leaves. Leaf mold muffled their steps and undergrowth kept the line of sight short. She could just glimpse Aren as he skirted a stand of young trees.

"I'm going forward to walk with Aren," she said to Benoia.

"Good luck with that." Then Benoia added, "Ask him how much farther we have to go."

chapter sixteen

ᚨᚱᛖN hᛖᚨᚱD ᛏhᛖ ᛋᚹiᚠᛏ soft footfalls approaching from behind and suppressed a groan. He'd known that Annikke wouldn't let it go. For the hundredth time that day he asked himself what Loki's whim had possessed him to tell her of his father's shame? And why couldn't he forget her foolish words?

Your father must have loved your mother very much.

He wanted to turn aside the bitter truth that if faced with a similar choice, he would make the same decision, but he couldn't.

I'm no better than my father.

Aren clenched his jaw. He refused to accept that. He might not have fulfilled his promise to protect Annikke, but he would *not* fail in his duty to the Jarl, or to his daughter.

Annikke caught up to him, only slightly out of breath from hurrying. Aren deliberately didn't look at her. If he didn't meet her eyes, maybe she wouldn't try to engage him in conversation. There really wasn't anything to say. He'd said more than enough last night.

"Before Benoia came to live with me I was used to people not talking to me. My parents didn't know what to say after I was Fey-marked, and the villagers—" She made a little noise of frustration. "There wasn't much point in trying. I was angry most of the time. Benoia changed me."

He wasn't going to ask how. If he didn't ask, she might return to Benoia's side, and leave him to the task of scouting the way ahead. And stewing in his own thoughts.

They walked a dozen steps in silence, and then a dozen more.

Is that all she's going to say?

"Benoia didn't see a Fey-marked woman," Annikke continued, "at least, not after we got used to each other. She didn't see my past; she just saw me. I, in turn, saw someone worth reaching out to. Someone worth letting into my heart. And then I realized that with a little effort on my part, some of the villagers might see me for who I am, and not just the color of my hair."

"I like your hair." *Gods, why did I say that?* It had just popped out. He couldn't stop himself; he stole a glance at her and was unexpectedly pleased to see he'd provoked a slight smile. Just as quickly, he pushed the feeling away.

A few steps later she added, "So now it bothers me again when people who should don't talk to me. I probably shouldn't care. But I do."

Hoder's hurl. What could he possibly say? He hadn't meant to hurt her, but he didn't want to talk about this either. He settled on simple honesty. "I'm sorry. I didn't mean to bring you grief."

"No—" She shook her head. "I mean yes, you grieved me, but it's my own fault. I was wrong, or at least not right. I can't imagine anything that might induce me to bring harm to Benoia, so your father's action is beyond my understanding. But I do know one thing; it had nothing to do with you. He made his decision for his own reasons. It had unintended results. At least I hope they were unintended, even though, in the end, his choice was a selfish one."

He knew Annikke's words were meant to help, but they stabbed deep.

"Don't. Just stop."

She opened her mouth, and then snapped it shut again.

Aren clenched his jaw tightly. He already knew his da had made a selfish choice. That was no comfort, because he knew now that he was just like his father.

Annikke gestured widely, lifting her hands with a jerk. "What did I say *this* time?"

He shook his head and looked away, into the trees. His heart jolted at what he saw there.

Bollocks! Aren pushed Annikke back behind him just before an arrow flew past where she'd been standing.

"Ware! Ware!" he shouted, as he swiftly nocked an arrow. "Get back!"

Annikke, bless her, didn't hesitate, but ducked behind a broad tree shouting, "We're being attacked!"

Aren had never been in combat beyond the occasional fist fight as a boy. The closest he'd ever come to dying was when the bear had charged him. Now, as then, time slowed while everything seemed to happen at once. Without conscious thought, he aimed and loosed his arrow.

It found its mark.

Aren barely took notice as he stepped to the side while pulling another shaft from his quiver. In the back of his mind he hoped that Vali had the sense to dismount, but with the forefront of his attention Aren was scanning the trees for his next target.

There. Another archer exposed himself as he drew down on Benoia, who was holding Pinter's headstall while Vali jumped from the saddle. Aren let fly at the man but his arrow thunked into a tree trunk. The man jumped at the sound; his shot went wide. Aren heard the thrum of another bowstring from behind him, and heard a sharp cry. He hoped that was Norva giving a good account of herself.

Behind Aren another man broke from cover. Aren heard the heavy footfalls and turned just in time to bring his bow down across his opponent's forearm with a crack. The man dropped the knife in that hand, and stumbled, but he carried a second blade. Aren shifted, barely preserving his manhood, but the knife sliced high across his thigh.

His leg collapsed.

Pain like nothing Aren had felt before lanced up into his groin. His assailant fell to his knees beside him, bent over the arm Aren had broken. He lifted his bloody knife to finish Aren, but the blow was prevented by Annikke throwing her body against the man's in a blur of green and silver. The man fell with a grunt, Annikke sprawled over him.

Aren tried to rise, to pull Annikke away before the man cut her, but the pain stole his breath. Before he could reach her, Annikke slammed her palm down on the earth. In an instant, the undergrowth they'd been fighting through half the day tangled itself around the other man's arms and legs. The warrior struggled, but couldn't move.

Before she could rise, another man broke from the trees heading directly for Annikke. He ran half crouched, holding his dagger low like an experienced fighter. At the last possible moment Annikke rolled away. The warrior followed. He only needed one step to reach her.

"*No!*" Suddenly Benoia was there, screeching, and hanging off the man's neck.

Aren expected the man to fling Benoia aside, or slice himself free of her grasp. Instead he gurgled, his eyes rolled back, and he toppled forward onto Annikke.

Benoia pulled and Annikke pushed, struggling the large man off of her. Annikke rose to hands and knees, then crawled to Aren's side. A second later she'd used the knife Aren's attacker had dropped to cut open Aren's trouser leg. She peeled the blood-soaked cloth back from his wound. He couldn't even bring himself to feel embarrassed as she examined his damaged flesh.

"No. Oh, no," she cried softly as she leaned into his wound with both hands.

Not the words a man wanted to hear the first time a woman beheld his naked self. Yet they only confirmed Aren's suspicion.

"Is it a mortal wound, or will I merely lose the leg?" he grated out as pain tore through his body.

Annikke didn't look at him. "You won't lose the leg."

He was going to die, then. This was not the fate he'd imagined for himself, but at least he'd fallen in combat. It was an honorable end, not like his father's, but Tandra would still be fatherless.

"Benoia, help me!" Annikke pressed harder against his groin and the agony of it tore a scream from his throat. He would have preferred to pass out, but the gods were not so generous. Warmth spread out from where Annikke was touching him, and he prayed to Thor that he hadn't pissed himself.

Movement drew his eye. Another archer had drawn his bow, his shaft aimed at Annikke, or possibly Benoia. Before Aren could shout a warning, the arrow flew.

"No!"

But Annikke's chest didn't sprout an arrowhead. Another shaft knocked the first from its path, and buried itself deeply in the trunk of a tree.

Oblivious, Annikke murmured words in a musical language, while Benoia, pale and shaking, stood behind her, gripping Annikke's shoulders as she put pressure on the slice in his flesh. The warmth in his groin spread throughout his body. Aren's pain throbbed in time with his speeding heart, gradually subsiding to a monstrous ache.

Aren wasn't sure if minutes or only seconds had passed when Annikke sat back on her heels, dropping her blood drenched hands into her lap. She blinked for a moment as though she couldn't quite focus.

Norva spoke from behind him. "Gods, that's a lot of blood! Will he live?"

Aren sat up and wrapped Annikke's fingers in his own. "Are you all right?"

Annikke took a moment before she came back to herself, then her gaze met his. "How do you feel?"

"I asked you first," he countered with half a grin, then he sobered. "I find myself unexpectedly alive, thanks to you."

"Good," Annikke said with a nod.

Behind her, Benoia plopped down gracelessly, wrapping her arms around herself as if she were cold.

Annikke slipped out of her pack's straps and helped Benoia to do the same before finding her cloak and draping it over the younger woman's shoulders. "Norva, would you build a fire? We won't be continuing today."

"Wait," Aren protested, starting to get to his feet. "We shouldn't stay here. How many of them were there, anyway?"

Norva easily pushed him back down with a hand

on his shoulder. "You've lost a lot of blood. If the Healer says you need to stay put, that's what we're going to do."

Vali came into view. "I count four dead, plus this one tied up by the weeds. Three arrow shot and one, well, I don't know what happened to him. "

Aren jerked his head up, looking for the archer whose arrow had been deflected in mid-flight. The woods were empty. "One of them got away. An archer." He pointed. "He shot from over there."

Norva nodded and trotted over to the spot where the man had taken aim. Then she disappeared into the trees.

"I'll build the fire," Vali said, and suited action to words.

Annikke sat next to Benoia and cuddled the shivering woman close.

"Is she all right?" Aren asked.

"She always gets the shakes after, a, uh, healing."

"But not you?"

Annikke shook her head. "No. I'm fine. Just tired." She looked where Aren had pointed, then followed the probable trajectory back to Aren. "Why isn't one of us dead?"

Norva reappeared and said, "Maybe his shot went wide. When I last saw him, he was running for his life. Something scared the piss out of him."

"That's what scared him." Aren indicated the arrow buried deeply in a tree to his left. "He saw the archer that let fly that shaft." The arrow, what stood out from the trunk, was smooth and straight, and fletched with purple feathers striped with gold. He'd seen that fletching before, when Torlon had saved his life with another impossible shot.

"Elves!" Annikke said.

"What?" Norva exclaimed.

Aren lifted his brows. He shouldn't be surprised

that she recognized the fletching. It was fairly obvious that Torlon's brother, Gaelon, was the Elf she'd once encountered. Why else would he concern himself with her welfare? Actually, why *would* he? Aren shook his head. That was a question not likely to ever be answered.

Vali's head came up as he brought the small fire to flame. His expression was alight with interest. "Elves?"

Annikke stood and shouted, "Come out! Show yourselves!" Her voice shook with anger. "Stop skulking in the shadows!"

"Whoa! Whoa!" Norva put a hand lightly over Annikke's mouth. "If there *are* Elves lurking, and I'd guess you would know, let them stay hidden! I don't want to return Lord Vali to his mother Fey-marked."

Annikke swept Norva's hand aside, and the Daughter of Freya tried to put a restraining hand on Annikke's arm.

Norva wasn't being rough, but Aren didn't like her trying to force her will on Annikke. "Let her be," he commanded. "Not every encounter with the Elves results in Fey-marking."

Norva, Vali, Benoia, and Annikke all turned wide eyes on him.

Frigga's fanny. Now he'd stepped in it. "No harm will come to Vali. Not from these Elves."

"You seem rather sure of that," Norva said.

"He's right," a voice said from the shadows. A moment later Gaelon and Torlon emerged from the forest's shadows. "We mean none of you any harm."

chapter seventeen

Annikke glared, meeting Gaelon's gaze. It had been five years since she'd last seen him. Five years since he'd said he'd leave her in peace.

"Hello, Annikke." He hadn't changed a whit. He still appeared to be the same careless youth who had stolen her so many years ago. He came closer, moving with such grace that he seemed to hardly touch the ground, and reached out to touch Benoia.

Annikke put out a hand to stop him, and Gaelon paused. "The magic is warring with her Talent. Let me help her."

Annikke hesitated, then nodded.

Gaelon laid his hand on Benoia's head and murmured briefly in that beautiful language that stirred a whisper of longing in Annikke's breast and made her heart clutch with fear. It wasn't healthy to hunger after something so *other*. She almost wished they hadn't given back her memories five years ago. She'd seen great beauty while among the Elves, but she did *not* want to return to live with them.

Benoia stopped shaking, and looked up with a steady gaze as the Elf stepped back. "Thank you," she said.

Gaelon smiled. "You're most welcome. You should be able to use the healing magic now without it harming you. But little one, you must be wary. It wasn't meant to harm."

"The first time it just happened. But even if I could have stopped it, what else could I have done? Should I have let him—"

"No. Never that," Gaelon said. "You have done harm thus far only in great need, but each time you do, it will grow easier. Use the magic to harm often, and it will eat your soul."

Tears welled and cascaded down Benoia's cheeks. "I know. I felt it." She inhaled a shuddering breath. "A part of me liked it," she whispered.

The Elf nodded solemnly. "You're strong. But be very, very careful from now on."

Annikke knelt and pulled Benoia into a hug. "Oh, sweetling."

"Are we forgiven?" Gaelon asked.

Annikke looked up into the Elf's face and sighed. Had she thought him unchanged from their first encounter? She'd been wrong. "For saving my life? For healing Benoia? Yes. I'm not so bitter I'd cast blame on you for that."

Gaelon's expression brightened. "Excellent! Thank you."

"Now that *that's* settled," the other Elf said, "will you introduce us to your other companions?"

"No!" Norva said.

"Yes," said Vali.

Annikke glanced from the Daughter of Freya to the young lord. She understood Norva's fear and her desire to keep Vali safe, but it was too late for that, now. "Lord Vali, may I present to you Gaelon and—I don't know your name, sir," she said to the other Elf.

The Fey half-bowed over a hand spread on his breast. "Torlon. A pleasure to meet you, Lord Vali."

Vali contained his excitement enough to bow the same amount in return. "I'm honored to meet representatives of our hosts here in Alfheim. Thank you for your hospitality."

Torlon, whom Annikke thought was the elder of the two, bowed again at Vali's courtesy.

Norva said nothing when she was introduced. She made a slight choking noise, and barely nodded her acknowledgement.

"And this is Aren. He's escorting me and Benoia to Quartzholm."

"We meet again, Aren."

He's had dealing with the Elves before? She'd suspected so from his earlier words, but he'd said nothing of it. Most people wouldn't, of course. But that didn't stop her from feeling slighted. He knew about her, after all.

Aren glanced quickly at Annikke as if to gage her reaction. Was that a glimmer of guilt in his eye? Then he inclined his head to Torlon.

"Welcome. Once again I am indebted to you for your prowess with the bow. What price will you ask of me this time?"

"Nonsense. There is no debt. I had no other target worthy of my skill," Torlon said with a slight smile playing about the corners of his mouth. "Or permitted to me, for that matter."

Aren sighed. "As you say."

Torlon's smile widened. "Indeed."

"And the archer who provided your target?" Aren asked. "Will he trouble us again, do you think?"

"Unlikely. He seemed disinclined to make our acquaintance."

Aren nodded. "Good. Let's hope he continues to feel that way. It's just as well you don't desire payment for another debt; I've done a poor job of paying the last one."

Torlon's smile faded and he glanced at Annikke. His close perusal of her made her want to squirm, but she held still and lifted her chin.

"What debt?" she asked.

"How so?" Torlon asked at the same time. "Annikke is alive and seems well."

"No thanks to me," Aren answered. "Norva and her companions saved her the first time these Loki's Snot came calling. You saved her this time."

Keeping me safe was payment for a debt to the Elves? Why? And how does that fit with his duty to the Jarl?

"That's true," Gaelon said. "It *was* your shot that saved her, Torlon. His debt remains unpaid."

"No, it doesn't!" Annikke objected. Whatever his faults, Aren shouldn't be tied to the Elves. No one should. "He was hunting at *my* request when those men came two days ago. Vali's in Emergence and needed food. Aren couldn't know we'd be in danger while he was gone. And he *did* save my life just now. He saw the archer before his first arrow flew and pulled me out of the way."

"And then, because you were busy saving my life, you and Benoia exposed yourselves to more danger!" Aren lifted his hands and raised his voice.

"Why are you diminishing your role in this?" Annikke shouted back. "If you hadn't spotted him, that bowman would have taken us unawares."

"Enough," Torlon said, a smirk twisting the corner of his mouth. "Annikke's need for protection still exists and you're yet a day from Quartzholm. There is ample opportunity for you to satisfy your debt."

"And why, exactly, do you want him to protect me?" Annikke demanded.

"Because he wouldn't go home and let us do it," Gaelon said.

"That's not an answer," Annikke snapped. Had the Elves always been so slippery with their explanations? "Why would you want to? Our dealings are done. You paid your debt to me five years ago."

Gaelon looked at Torlon who lifted a brow. "The payment of my debt to you has brought you yet more grief."

Torlon nodded. "His debt to you is greater today than it was five summers ago."

"That's nonsense!" Annikke said.

"You'd be happier if Sveyn had raped me because I couldn't defend myself?" Benoia demanded sharply.

"At least his injury wouldn't be on our heads," Torlon answered.

Benoia took a swift step forward and slapped the Elf. "It's not on *your* head you smug, self-involved little weasel! It's on mine! *I* shriveled Sveyn's miserable little cock. You can run back to wherever you came from with a clear conscience. It's *my* fault that Annikke has been driven from her home."

There was a moment of stunned silence as Annikke and the others took in the fact that Benoia had offered violence to one of the Fey. Tears coursed down the girl's cheeks but she seemed unaware of them. Annikke rose and put her arms around her foster-daughter. "Please forgive her. She's endured so much these last days. She didn't mean—"

Torlon smiled ruefully, rubbing the side of his face. "It is forgotten. Compared to the blow an Elf maiden would deliver, it was a caress."

Then Norva said, "You're wrong, Benoia. Sveyn's injury isn't on your head, it's on his own."

"That's a lovely sentiment, and I appreciate the thought, but Lord Tholvar is still after us," Benoia said in a tone that suggested that Norva had missed an obvious point.

"Thus your need for protection," Gaelon said. "And whether or not your action was justified, you could not have taken it but for me and the magic I gave you. I share responsibility."

"Wonderful. You can come to Quartzholm and tell Lord Dahleven that," Annikke snapped. "But Aren won't be traveling for several days. I did my best, but his injury needs time to heal."

Again the Elves exchanged a glance. "That's something we can help with, if you will allow it," Gaelon asked Aren.

Annikke saw the struggle on his face, and knew he didn't want to be any more indebted to the Fey than he already was.

When he spoke, Aren's tone was resigned. "It wouldn't be prudent to camp here in the forest while I recover enough to travel. That archer might rediscover his courage. In the interest of being better able to protect Annikke and Benoia, and of seeing them safely to Quartzholm as soon as possible, I accept your offer."

Torlon chuckled. "Yes, of course. This won't incur new obligation. We do it only to assist you in paying your debt."

Gaelon knelt beside Aren. Annikke watched and listened carefully as the Elf put his hands over the wound. With the Elves' unexpected arrival, no one, not even Aren, had thought to cover his nakedness. His spilt blood had congealed and dried on his muscular thigh, and now that she wasn't concerned with saving his life, Annikke couldn't help notice his exposure, seeing him as a man rather than a patient. Even as a healer, she'd seen few men's privates. Feeling her face flood with heat, she looked away and met Norva's gaze. The older woman waggled her eyebrows in appreciation.

Annikke had never played the casual love games of youth. None of the village boys had wanted to test their luck with a Fey-marked girl, so she didn't know if Aren was exceptional or not. Norva seemed to think so, however.

Then the Elf began murmuring in his song-like tongue and Norva lost her smirk as she blanched and turned away, muttering a soft curse and a prayer for protection. Annikke smiled. At least the other woman wasn't staring at Aren's cock anymore.

A few minutes later Gaelon sat back. "You'll be sore, but you can safely travel to Quartzholm now. We should move away from this place of death. Have you another pair of trews?"

Aren grimaced. "Nay. I didn't think I'd have need."

"I can mend them," Annikke said, "but I'll not be able to get the blood out of them."

Aren swore. "I don't welcome the comments that will come of walking into Quartzholm with my crotch drenched in blood."

Torlon laughed. "I can help with that. I'll put a bit of glamor on them that will last long enough for you to change. No one will be alarmed on that score."

"You're coming with us to Quartzholm?" Vali asked, the eagerness plain in his voice.

"We'll see you safe to only to the edge of the village," Torlon said to Norva, who had an alarmed expression. "We don't want to call your sanity into question," he finished with wry tone.

chapter eighteen

ᴀʀᴇɴ ᴡᴀᴛᴄʜᴇᴅ ᴀɴɴɪᴋᴋᴇ plying her needle on the slashes in his trews. When their group moved, they left the one man still living held fast to the ground by the weeds. The Elves had reinforced Annikke's command, but they said he'd work his way free by the next day. Torlon had leaned close to the man's face and warned him of the danger of pursuing them too closely.

Their attacker had wet his pants.

The dead they'd left like Outcasts, lying untended on the ground where they'd fallen. The Elves refused to spend a moment's time on men who'd tried to kill Annikke and Benoia, and Aren felt much the same, even though one of those men was dead because of him.

Aren turned the thought over in his mind. A man would not return to his family because Aren's arrow had found its mark. He'd never killed a man before, and he didn't much like the feeling. But he couldn't wish he'd done otherwise. Annikke and Benoia's lives had been in peril.

It was still light when they'd made a new camp, and Annikke had bent to the task of mending his clothing. Aren imagined her sewing in a rocking chair in front of a cozy fire in his cottage. Head bent over her work, she was unmindful of the silver strands that had come loose from her braid. He wanted to tuck them behind her ear, much as he would have with Tandra.

No, not at all like he would with his daughter. He wanted to brush Annikke's hair back and kiss the delicate ear he'd expose, and on down her neck to her collarbone, and then lay her down on his bed and wrap himself around her. He wanted to feel the silver beauty of her hair trailing over his skin, and tease her nipples with the soft tail of her own braid.

His cock began to stiffen, despite his blood loss.

What in Freya's name am I thinking!

There was no future to be had with this woman. She and Benoia were fugitives, and he was taking them to face Lord Dahleven's justice. That was all there could ever be between them. He hoped the Jarl would see that Benoia had only defended herself, but the girl had harmed the heir of a lord, a lord whose vote the Jarl needed at the upcoming Althing, the annual meeting of the Jarls and their lords. A man might think of his own daughter, sister, and wife facing assault and treat Benoia with compassion, but a Jarl who wanted to enfranchise all women in his province might think their needs outweighed those of a single girl.

Even worse, Benoia had used Elven magic.

Was doing so a violation of the Laws of Sanction? Aren didn't know. Most would think so, even if it wasn't. Lord Dahleven might have the support to make an unpopular decision, but would he spend it by deciding in favor of the foster-daughter of a Fey-marked woman? Shame twisted Aren's gut. He hadn't set out to deceive Annikke and Benoia, or himself, for that matter. Nevertheless, he'd led the women to believe the Jarl would be sympathetic to them, and though he might well be, Aren knew that sympathy wasn't likely to translate to leniency for the girl.

Afternoon sun filtered through the trees, sparking light from Annikke's hair. The magic of it couldn't distract Aren from the miserable truth.

Taking Benoia back to Quartzholm was very probably going to bring grief to Annikke, and he couldn't imagine she'd want anything to do with him after that. Worse, he'd be breaking his promise to Torlon. Again.

"Why are you staring at her like that?"

Benoia's low challenge startled Aren into speaking the truth. "Because she's beautiful."

In a tone that wouldn't be overheard, Benoia declared, "She's more than beautiful. She's honorable and compassionate."

Aren smiled at Benoia's fierce defense of her foster-mother. "I can see that. I wish my daughter had so devoted a mother."

The young woman's brow furrowed as she considered his answer. "You aren't put off by her being Feymarked?"

"Why should I be?" Aren replied in a similarly low voice. "She's clearly not mad. And I've had dealings with the Elves myself, after all."

"Then what are you going to do about it?" Rather than sounding like she was afraid he'd take advantage of her foster-mother, Benoia's tone suggested impatience with his lack of action.

Taken aback, Aren asked, "What do you propose?"

Benoia shrugged. "Free me from my parole. Let me go, if not to Forsvaremur with Norva and Lord Vali, then somewhere else. I'll be safe from Sveyn and his father, and your generosity will earn you Annikke's gratitude."

Aren wished his choice could be that simple and straightforward. The idea of letting Benoia go, and of having Annikke, warm and loving in his arms each night was tempting—and that seductive whisper scared him more than standing on the edge of a precipice. He owed his life to Torlon, and that debt preceded the oaths made to Lord Fender and the Jarl. He could do as Benoia asked, fulfill his promise to the Elf, and have Annikke.

Was this how Da broke his oath to his liege? By putting sentiment over duty?

Shame would follow his daughter for the rest of her life if he failed his duty to Lord Fender.

What would the Elves do if he helped others bring grief and harm to Benoia and Annikke? He had no idea, but he didn't think they'd visit their wrath upon his family. Tandra would be safe—but what kind of man would he be if he allowed that to happen?

Aren huffed a bitter laugh. "An excellent argument, but for two small problems. One, Annikke might be grateful, but she'd leave with you, not cleave to me."

Benoia bowed her head. "And what is the second?"

Freyr protect me. "My duty to Lord Dahleven will not allow it."

Aren hoped he wasn't trading shame for Elven retribution.

The sun was fully up when they set out for Quartzholm the next morning. Annikke was happy to see that Aren didn't even have a limp.

He caught her staring as he tested his movement and smiled. "Nearly good as new, thanks to you."

Annikke dropped her gaze, but it was too late. She

was already blushing. "And Gaelon."

"Aye." Aren sounded resigned.

The Elves accompanied them to where the road escaped the forest, and put a temporary glamour on Aren's pants so the blood stain wouldn't draw attention.

"You still have your debt to pay," Torlon reminded him.

"I well know it," Aren replied.

Annikke shook her head and made a derisive noise. "How many times does he have to save my life before his debt is paid?"

Torlon kept staring into Aren's eyes as he answered her. "As many times as necessary."

As they approached the edge of the village that surrounded the wall around Quartzholm, the size of the place seemed to grow. This was far larger than Lord Tholvar's manor. Annikke had never seen so many people in one place, not even on festival days in her village. She tried not to gape and stare as Aren led their group up one of the main thoroughfares through the town that spilled down the slope outside castle walls. All morning and through the afternoon, Annikke had tried to imagine what Quartzholm would be like, but even Aren's description had not prepared her.

Rising high on the skirts of the mountain beyond, rose quartz walls rose dozens of feet above the granite curtain wall that separated the castle from the one and two story stone buildings of the village. Several people called out greetings to Aren as their group climbed the switch-backed avenue and he responded with a few words or a smile and a wave.

Finally they faced the massive gates that stood wide open like a giant maw waiting to swallow them.

Her foster daughter stopped and stood rigidly staring. Annikke took her hand. "Courage, sweetling. I'm with you."

Benoia swallowed hard, and then lifted a brow at Annikke. "You only call me that when things are really bad."

Annikke blinked. Was that true?

"It's all right. I don't need to hear it every day." Benoia squeezed Annikke's hand. "Your heart isn't hidden." She straightened her shoulders, and they continued through the gates into the courtyard.

The paved bailey was big enough to accommodate ten of the village marketplaces back home. From where she stood Annikke could see three towers punctuating the buttressed walls. Catwalks connected them near the top, and staircases ran up to each in between. More towers connected by arching spans marked the castle that seemed to grow out of the mountains. It loomed over them like a massive hammer about to fall.

A wide staircase led up to an entrance flanked by several guardsmen. Aren identified himself, and then introduced Lord Vali and Norva. "Lord Vali is in Emergence. Escort him to suitable rooms, summon a Healer and *stirkedrikk*, and let the Jarl know Lady Solveig's son is our guest."

Vali threw Annikke a wry glance as the guardsmen reacted with the exactly right level of concern. Annikke could see that neither he nor Aren noticed the glances at her hair, or the looks passing between the guards.

Aren waited until Lord Vali and Norva had disappeared within before saying, "This is Annikke Torrsonsdatter and Benoia Fornosdatter. They'll also need appropriate lodging."

Annikke watched the guard's face turn hard, and her heart faltered.

"You captured the Fey-marked witch and her fledgling? Well done. We'll take charge of them." One of the guards grasped Annikke's upper arm tightly while another pulled Benoia over to him with similar roughness.

"Get yourself some food."

"These women have given me their parole," Aren objected, putting a restraining hand on the man's arm. "Treat them with courtesy."

The guard stiffened, and jerked free of Aren's grasp with a sharp twist.

Annikke's heart picked up speed. This wasn't what Aren had said would happen. Too late, instinct urged her to flee. She took half a step away but the guard roughly jerked her back.

"Are you Fey-marked, too? These *prisoners* are dangerous and have a warrant sworn on them."

A warrant?

The shock on Aren's face told Annikke all she needed to know. He hadn't lied to her, but that mattered little now. The Jarl had already made up his mind. Would he have them stripped of their Talents? Exiled? She should have let Benoia run instead of encouraging her to trust the Jarl's justice.

"Sworn by who?" Aren demanded.

The guard answered with a disgusted sneer. "It's none of my concern who brought the charges. I obey my captain's orders and he obeys the Jarl. And *the Jarl* wants the prisoners detained until he sees fit to hear their case."

A small spurt of hope diluted Annikke's fear. *At least Lord Dahleven still intends to hear Benoia's side.*

"When was that order given?"

"Yesterday."

Annikke searched Aren's face, wondering why that mattered. "What does this mean?"

Aren ran a hand over his beard. "The Jarl sent me to bring you in to give your account of what happened. When I left, Lord Tholvar had brought a complaint but a warrant hadn't been sworn on you. Matters have progressed in the sevenday I've been gone."

"Maybe the men who escaped came here and brought new accusations," Benoia said.

"Enough chatter," the first guard said. "Come with us."

The guards marched Annikke and Benoia down a stair and through smooth stone hallways lit by glow-lights. Annikke's heart sank. The Jarl must be powerful if even his prison enjoyed the luxury of Talent generated light. What hope had she of persuading him of Benoia's innocence, and her vulnerability to Sveyn's unwanted attention, if he'd never known any himself?

Annikke heard Aren following but the guard gripping her arm hustled her and Benoia along briskly and she couldn't turn to see him. The passage turned several times, until they came to a room with a table and chairs. Two men sat there, playing bones.

"What have we here?" one asked.

"Annikke Torsonsdatter and Benoia Fornosdatter. Warranted, both of them. They're to be kept separate."

Separate! Annikke turned to the guard who was still tightly clasping her upper arm. After all Benoia had been through, Annikke didn't want her to be alone. "No! Please, put us together."

One of the new guards laughed nastily. "Why? Are you two lovers like those Daughters of Freya? I could teach you better."

Her escort pulled Annikke back from the leering guard and pushed her into the custody of his companion. Annikke clung to Benoia as the man who'd left marks on her arm turned to loom over the guard, but Aren was already in his face.

"Listen very closely," Aren said in a voice as hard as the granite walls. "The Jarl does not tolerate abuse of prisoners, and Lord Fender takes great pleasure in disciplining those who do. Harm them at your peril."

The guard lifted his nose. "You're not my commander."

Aren bared his teeth in a humorless grin. "No. I just play bones with him."

The guard backed up a step, bumping into Annikke's escort who stood just behind. "Fine. I was just making a joke. There's no *harm* in that." He shot a narrow-eyed glance at her and Benoia as if he blamed them for the set-down he'd just received. A chill shivered down Annikke's spine. She didn't want Benoia in this man's care.

Her foster-daughter shook as she had after Sveyn's attack, but the girl wasn't weeping now. Anger burned in Benoia's eyes. "The last man who tried to rape me got a shriveled cock for his trouble," she snarled at the guard, "so don't even think about it."

"Benoia!" Annikke rebuked her foster-daughter out of habit, but she couldn't keep a smile from the corner of her mouth as the man paled. It probably wasn't wise to provoke someone like him, but she couldn't bring herself to fault her foster-daughter.

The guards escorted them into a long hallway punctuated with metal doors. One of the guards took Benoia to the far end, while Annikke's held open a door near their break room. They wouldn't even be able to hear each other.

Annikke paused in the doorway of her cell. A sliver of light filtered down from a horizontal slot near the ceiling, giving just enough illumination to see how meager her accommodations were. The cell held only a narrow sleeping bench cut into the stone wall, covered with a thin straw mattress and a rough wool blanket. At least all appeared clean, even if a malodorous bucket sat in the corner.

This was what she'd counseled Benoia to come to Quartzholm for? This was the Jarl's justice?

"Get in there." The guard shoved her in and shut

the solid iron door. It rang with finality as it locked behind her.

The guards stopped Aren from following them down the hallway to the cells. He wanted to defy them, but it would serve no purpose, so he forced himself to wait at the entry point. His gut churned as he watched the women being locked away, all the while trying to not imagine how Annikke's worry for the girl must be weighing on her. He understood the woman well enough after only these few days to know that she wouldn't be thinking of her own danger. Annikke was a truer mother to Benoia, even though they weren't blood, than his daughter's mother had been to her.

That alone was the source of his admiration for her. That and her willingness to expose her Elven gifts by healing him. It wasn't because she was beautiful, or that he wanted her in his bed.

Annikke glanced back at him. Glowlights glinted on her hair. She took his breath away, even tired and bedraggled, with wisps of silver coming loose from her braid.

"Try not to worry," he said, sounding lame to his own ears.

Her smile was weak, but she nodded.

Aren watched as the women who'd been in his charge were caged, and then turned on his heel and left.

Over the last several days he'd worried about becoming an Oathbreaker, about whether the Jarl would judge Benoia harshly for what, in Aren's opinion, was her fully justified defense of self. On more than one occasion he'd been horrified by the close margin by which Annikke and her daughter had been kept from harm. He respected Annikke's strength and caring, and saw more than a little of his daughter in Benoia. They should have been confined under watch in servants' quarters, not in the *gaol*. That was generally used only for murderers and violent men who refused to give their parole. Lord Fender would never have allowed this.

Where is *Lord Fender?*

Aren stalked through the polished stone passages of the castle, unseeing. He'd managed to keep his word to both Lord Dahleven and Torlon, but only just barely. Annikke and Benoia were in Quartzholm and safe. Now all he had to do was keep them so.

chapter nineteen

smells of dinner cooking wafted into the street from the cottages Aren passed on his way home. He looked forward to eating his mother's stew and sleeping in his own bed again, but the pleasure of his anticipation was muted. Annikke and Benoia would be eating prisoner's fare and sleeping in bleak cells.

Tandra looked up from the onions she was chopping as he entered. "Da! You're back!" She jumped up to greet him as his mother turned to smile. Halfway across the room Tandra's face assumed an expression of horror. "You're hurt!"

"Summon a Healer!" his mother exclaimed. "Quick girl!"

Aren looked down at the front of his trews. The Elves' glamour had faded and the stain now showed clearly that he'd lost a lot of blood. He caught his daughter by the arm before she ran out the door. "It's all right. I'm not hurt." He pulled first his daughter and then his mother into a big hug, rubbing their backs.

His mother pulled away first, her brows knitting as she glanced down at his recently mended pants. "There's a tale here, clearly. But first you should bathe and change."

"Aye," Aren agreed.

A candlemark later Aren returned from the public baths clean and freshly clothed. In the interest of keeping his mother and daughter from worrying, he told them a falsehood—that the blood staining his pants belonged to another man who'd tried to hurt Annikke. Then he diverted their attention by relating his rescue of Vali.

Tandra listened eagerly and wondered aloud if she might see the young lord before he returned to Forsvaremur. In return, she related all the goings on in the castle that she'd heard while he was gone.

Aren listened with only half an ear to his daughter's account. It warmed his heart to be back home with his family, and Tandra's happiness reassured him that his decision to uproot them all and bring them here to Quartzholm had been a good one. But as Aren watched his daughter wash the dishes, his thoughts kept straying to Annikke and Benoia. Annikke had sacrificed her home and come to Quartzholm with little choice in the matter, and she wasn't enjoying her evening meal with Benoia or with much hope of a better future.

"Goodnight, Da." Tandra kissed his cheek. "I'm glad you're back." Then she climbed into the loft where she slept.

For a few minutes he and his mother sat in silence except for the slight creak of her rocking chair. A summer breeze wafted through the open shutters, carrying wisps of domestic sounds from other cottages on the lane. He was home again with his family, but Aren couldn't be restful. He stood and paced over to the still damp dishes, taking a towel to them instead of letting them air dry.

It wasn't right that Annikke and Benoia should be treated so harshly, and had Lord Fender been in the castle he would not have allowed it. But even his commander couldn't gainsay a warrant. The women were as safe as they could be in the gaol. Aren was sure the guard understood the risks of abusing them and would leave them alone. Yet safe or not, he knew Annikke was afraid for Benoia, and Aren had brought her into that fearful place.

"What troubles you?" his mother asked, drawing him out of his thoughts.

"What makes you think I'm troubled?"

His mother rolled her eyes, but said nothing.

Aren laughed mirthlessly. His mother was no fool. She knew him. He'd just returned from a long journey and yet he was pacing and drying dishes for no good reason.

"The women I escorted to Quartzholm are honorable women, but I fear things will not go well for them. There's an angry lord looking for vengeance, and they have no man to speak for them."

"You're a good man to think of them, son, but this is clearly not your problem."

"It is."

His mother lifted a brow. "How so?"

He sought for a way to answer without telling her about the Elves and his debt to Torlon. A debt he was in danger of defaulting on. He'd never told her that an Elf had saved his life those many years ago. He hadn't wanted to frighten her with the truth that she'd almost lost her only son, especially at a time when most folk feared the Fey. He'd been his mother's only support, so he hadn't wanted to burden her with the knowledge. Now he couldn't explain his debt without revealing his secret.

Aren sat again. "I promised a friend of theirs that I'd keep them safe."

Dismay filled his mother's expression. "Why would you do such a foolish thing?"

In response Aren asked a question too long left silent, a question that had been much on his mind this last week. "Why did Da not answer Lord Fellig's call?"

Hurt replaced dismay on his mother's face, chased away by ... *guilt*?

"That ship passed downriver long ago. Why bring it up now?"

"Tell me, Mother."

A spark of anger flashed in her eyes, but she quickly looked away. "Because I asked him to stay with me."

Aren's mouth fell open. "You asked Da to break his oath?"

"I was afraid I was going to die. Afraid your da would die in Fellig's stupid raids and leave me alone with a son to raise. I loved him so much, and I didn't want to lose him. Didn't want you to be fatherless. Or if I died, an orphan."

"And yet he left us anyway."

His mother shook her head. "It was my fear that killed your da. He loved me more than he should, and he stayed with me because I asked it of him. But he was a good man. An honorable man. He couldn't bear the shame of being an Oathbreaker. I think he thought if he was dead, he'd take the shame of what he'd done to the grave with him. He never meant to saddle you with it. Never wanted you to suffer for his choice. You know that, don't you?"

No I don't know that.

Memories of his da *before* came flooding back. Memories Aren had kept walled away, because it hurt too much to remember what he'd lost. His da teaching him to draw a bow, to plow a straight furrow, to mend harness. Laughter shared over the evening meal. Aren stared at the last few embers that glowed in the hearth as anger and shame and love roiled in his gut.

Aren ran a hand over his beard. "I do know that. But his shame still clings to this family, even if he never wanted it to. I brought us here to earn some honor, for you, for Tandra. And now I'm cross-sworn, just as Da was."

Cross-sworn. He'd fulfilled one oath at the cost of the other. He'd told himself there was nothing he could do about it, but there was. He just didn't like it.

Aren slipped from his chair to kneel at his mother's knee, gently taking her work worn hands in his. "Ma, I uprooted you and Tandra and brought us here to make things better."

"You made a good choice. The Healers here are helping me. I feel better than I have in years, and Tandra is happy here. She'll be able to choose a good husband, to have a better future."

Aren winced. Everything his mother said was true. And it made his next words even harder to say. "I need to do something for those women I brought to Quartzholm. I'm sorry, Mother, but this will likely make things worse for us." He looked away. "I'm no better than Da was."

"You could do a great deal worse!" His mother's expression was fierce. "Your da chose family over all. You should do the same. Think of me! Think of Tandra! Those women aren't family. You owe them nothing. They're strangers."

"I owe Annikke my life, Mother."

"What do you mean?"

"The blood on my pants. It wasn't my opponent's. It was mine. Annikke saved me, and put herself in harm's way to do it."

"After you saved her, no doubt. Your debts are balanced. No one would say differently."

No one would. Not even Annikke.

"Think of your daughter, son."

He lifted his gaze to meet that of the woman who'd given him life, who'd extracted a soul-killing promise from his father. "Tandra's future and whether she marries or not is in the Norns' weaving. More important is that she respects her da. And I must respect myself for that to happen."

A creak on the ladder to the loft brought Aren's head around. Tandra stood there in her nightrail, her hair free from its braids. She might be his little girl, but she was already on the road to being a woman. A woman whose future would be affected by the choices he made, whatever he'd said to his mother about fate.

Tandra climbed down the last few steps. "I've always felt safe because you were there. Those women are alone, Da. Do what you must. Whatever happens, Grandmother and I will be fine, as we've always been."

"Girl, this is your future you're tossing to the wayside! You don't know what you're saying," his mother exclaimed.

"I do," Tandra said, meeting Aren's gaze.

Throat tight with emotion, Aren gave his daughter a swift, hard, hug and then left, snagging two cloaks from the pegs by the door as he passed into the night.

It was late in the night and Annikke's cell was blacker than the bottom of a cooking pot when she heard the gate to the guard room open. She guessed that several candlemarks had passed since one of the guards had slipped a bowl of warm porridge through the slot at the bottom of the door. There was no reason for anyone to be in the hall until morning. Had Aren's warning fallen on deaf ears? Were the guards coming after all, to use her and Benoia for their pleasure? Annikke's heart raced as if struggling to escape.

Footsteps paused outside her cell. A key scraped as it penetrated the lock of her door. Could she defend herself as Benoia had done? Should she? Or would it be better to endure what was about to happen so as not to bring more wrath down upon them?

Annikke held her breath in the dark, waiting for the key to turn, the door to open, begging Baldur that no further harm would be visited upon her foster-daughter.

Something heavy thumped against her door, and she jumped. There were sounds of scuffling and a grunt of pain. Running footsteps receded.

Long moments passed and Annikke held her breath, as a key scraped in the lock of her door. She tensed, ready to fight without a second thought. Whatever the cost to her, she couldn't be passive.

Annikke blinked as the dim illumination from a glowlight poured into her cell.

The man standing there wasn't the guard who'd leered at Benoia. It wasn't the other guard either.

"Annikke?" Benoia's voice called faintly from her cell down the hall.

Aren held out a shaking hand to Annikke. His other hand held a bloody dagger. "It's all right. He's gone. Come with me."

Annikke blinked, took a deep shuddering breath. A moment later she rushed the three steps across her cell and into his arms. He pulled her close, wrapping her tightly in his strength. Nothing had felt so good. Then he pushed her back from him a little, looking her over. "Are you all right?"

Annikke laughed, but it came out sounding a bit hysterical. She swallowed, trying to regain a measure of calm. "Fine. I'm fine." Her eyes fastened on Aren's bloody blade. *Oh gods! He hasn't killed the guards has he?* "What have you done?"

"Saved your life, I think." Aren followed her gaze, then wiped his dagger clean on the thin blanket.

"Annikke!" Benoia's tone was frantic.

"Come on, sweetheart. Let's get the two of you out of here." Aren pulled the key from the lock and led her down the hallway to Benoia's cell. "I'll explain once you're safe."

Sweetheart? Annikke shook her head. Aren was just trying to settle her. *He meant nothing by it.*

Aren released Benoia, and her foster-daughter fell into her arms. After too short an embrace he hustled them out through the guards' room. The two men stood there facing the outer door, slack-jawed and unseeing. One had a hand outstretched as if in greeting.

"What's wrong with them?" Benoia asked.

"I don't know," Aren said. "I found them this way, and a man who had no business here was about to unlock Annikke's cell. He drew steel when he saw me, then fled when I cut him."

Annikke noticed the splatters of blood on the floor. "A Talent for creating a waking sleep, perhaps?"

"Maybe. Let's not linger. I don't want to explain what I'm doing here to these guards." He snagged two well-worn cloaks from the table, handed one to Benoia, and draped the other across Annikke's shoulders. "Pull the hoods forward to hide your faces."

Now that she was calmer, Annikke saw that Aren had bathed and changed clothes, while she was still dirty and smelly from their journey. She felt color rising in her cheeks, remembering how she'd flung herself into his arms. Annikke's eyes met his as he lifted the hood over her head and was surprised by the flash of warmth she saw there.

Just as quickly, it was gone and she wondered if she'd imagined it. Aren went to the door and peeked out, then almost pushed them out into the corridor before he latched the iron-bound door behind them. "I don't know how long the guards' condition will last or if they'll remember what happened, but I want to be well away before they wake or the next shift finds them."

"Where are you taking us?" Benoia whispered.

"Someplace safer than the gaol," Aren said. Then, in a soft voice Annikke barely heard, he added, "I hope."

chapter twenty

ΛREN FORCED himself to stride confidently as he escorted the women through castle passages while fearing they'd be stopped and questioned at every turning. The night was well advanced and there were few people to see them climbing stairs shaped from onyx or passing through the wide hallways decorated with intricately carved wooden doors. Those still about were the occasional guard and the runners positioned to fetch or carry messages.

As he guided the women down the hallway, Aren nodded to the guard standing watch near the stair as if the three of them belonged there. He rapped twice on Lord Vali's door.

After a short wait, Norva opened it, hair rumpled from sleep. Her brows lifted in surprise.

Aren spoke before she could, pitching his voice so the guard wouldn't overhear. "Please, don't ask questions." In a louder tone he added, "I've brought the companionship Lord Vali requested." He brazenly swept into Vali's suite, Benoia and Annikke following.

Norva shut the ornately carved door before beginning her scold. "Are you Fey-marked? Lord Vali didn't ask for bedwarmers—" Then Annikke and Benoia pushed back their hoods and the Daughter of Freya snapped her mouth shut on her diatribe. "No offense intended, mistress."

Annikke gave the Daughter of Freya a wry smile. "None taken."

"Annikke? Aren?" Vali emerged from an adjoining room, tying a robe closed around his waist. "What are you doing here?"

"I'm happy to see you are much recovered, my lord," Annikke said.

"Lord Dahleven's Healer, Helbreden, is quite competent, though after your care his bed-side manner left much to be desired." Vali made a face. "I had to drink more *stirkedrikk* before he'd leave me be." Vali paused and speared Aren with a sharp glance. "But somehow I don't think you've come just to check up on me."

"No, my lord," Aren said. "I'm here to beg a boon of you." He quickly outlined what had happened to Annikke and Benoia since they parted on the castle steps. "Will you give them sanctuary until time for the hearing, my lord?"

"You want to hide them *here*?" Norva exclaimed. "Lord Vali is a guest of the Jarl. What you ask puts him in a difficult position."

"Norva, enough." Vali's hands fisted at his sides and his mouth was tight. "I'm more than a little surprised that Lord Dahleven ordered them confined to the gaol, but I can't grant you any favors."

Aren's heart stopped. He had no second choice of a safe place to hide the women. He couldn't endanger his mother and daughter by taking Annikke and Benoia to his own home. It would be the first place both the assassin and the guards would look for them. Aren opened his mouth to protest, to beg if necessary, but Vali lifted a hand for silence in the manner of someone who expected to be obeyed.

"—Not when I and my house are still in your debt. I will gladly shelter the women who saved my life, but I won't subvert Lord Dahleven's justice."

"I'm not asking you to, my lord. I just want the women to arrive at their hearing alive."

"That I can do," Vali said.

"Thank you, my lord." Benoia curtsied.

Vali growled. "None of that."

Benoia flinched at his angry tone and Annikke put an arm around the younger woman's shoulders.

"What I mean is, after what you've done for me, you needn't 'my lord' me or curtsy or any of that," Vali said in a gentler voice.

"Thank you, my lord." Aren bowed, but couldn't keep his lips from curling into a smile.

Vali glared at him, and then laughed. "I suppose this pup shouldn't try to teach an old dog a new trick."

Aren's smile broadened. "Just so, my lord." Then he sobered. "There's one more thing. You can't tell anyone they're here."

"Why not?" Norva demanded. "Surely the Jarl can be trusted."

"I agree," Vali said, "but every castle has ears and wagging tongues. I'm sure I can come up with some tale to explain the two lovely but shy women in my suite. But I'll keep this secret only until the hearing."

Aren nodded. "Agreed. And as for that explanation, I've already led the guard to believe I brought a randy young lord some entertainment. Now it's time for me to go. I'll arrange for word to be sent when the women are to appear before Lord Dahleven."

Vali nodded. "I'll keep them safe."

Annikke stopped Aren with a hand on his arm before he got to the door. "Thank you. A thousand times, thank you. You're an honorable man, and kind. Your daughter's mother was a fool."

Annikke's words, her touch on his arm, lightened Aren's soul more than they should. He smiled down at her and put his hand over hers. "Thank you."

Norva cleared her throat, waiting with her hand on the door latch. Annikke blushed and looked away. "I shouldn't keep you."

Aren's attention snapped back to the tasks at hand, and said, "I should go," at the same time.

They shared an awkward smile and Aren turned to leave.

"Ladies, I have a private bath, if you'd like to avail yourselves of it." Vali said as Norva let Aren out of the suite.

Benoia squealed, "Yes! Yes!" just as the door closed behind him.

The guard posted at the stair turned at the noise, met Aren's gaze, and smirked.

Annikke followed Norva down a short passage. The smaller woman opened a door and steam billowed out. "Take as long as you need. I'll see what can be done about finding you some clean clothing."

"An indoor bathing room!" Benoia sighed as she stepped inside.

"Have you eaten?" Norva asked as Annikke turned to go in.

"They fed us," Benoia said in a tone that communicated her dislike of the fare.

Annikke thought of the meatless, unsalted porridge

her stomach had been too tense to accept and couldn't blame the girl for her tone. She shook her head. "No."

"We'll have something for you when you're done." She made a shooing motion with her hands. "In with you."

An attendant waited for them. She took their grimy clothes from them as they disrobed, touching the garments as little as possible, and directed them to stand on a grate under the sluice that came out of the wall. After rinsing the worst of the road grime from her skin, Annikke stepped into the large tub and perched on one of the benches, sinking into the deliciously hot water up to her collarbones. A constant flow of water streamed into the tub that was large enough for at least six people.

The warmth sank into Annikke's bones, melting away the knots in her muscles. She leaned back against the polished stone and closed her eyes. They couldn't know what they might face tomorrow, but for the moment, she felt glorious.

Benoia sighed beside her. "I never want to leave."

A haze of relaxation pushed the worry from Annikke's mind as she half floated in the steaming water. She could almost pretend that she had no worries and the future was bright.

The attendant spoke, "Ma'am?" and reality abruptly returned. The woman was holding out a back brush and a pot of soap.

Several minutes later, Annikke and Benoia had scrubbed and rinsed, then dried themselves with towels as soft as any Annikke had enjoyed during her time with the Elves. She'd heard that the Jarl had made an alliance with the Fey, but by the time news reached a small village like hers, rumor could turn black to white. As Annikke wrapped the fluffy fabric around her she thought the rumor might be true.

Such an agreement wouldn't influence the Jarl's

decision regarding Benoia. Men of power based their choices on what increased their influence over other men of power. But if Lord Dahleven was open to negotiating with the Elves, he might not hold Annikke's being Fey-marked against her foster-daughter.

Or so Annikke hoped.

chapter twenty-one

INSTEAD OF RETURNING home, Aren woke the
Commander of the Guard. It would only be a matter of
time before Hahlf summoned him. Once the men guarding the gaol awoke from their Talent induced daze
they'd report the missing prisoners. If they couldn't remember what happened, a Talent that could read the
recent history of a place would be called for. Aren's
presence would be noted. He might as well be the first to
tell the tale.

"You had better have an outstanding reason for
pulling me away from my lady wife," Hahlf barked. The
guardsman Aren had ordered to wake the commander
looked relieved that Hahlf's ire was now directed at
Aren and not himself.

"I do," Aren answered, and related an account of
the dazed guards and the would-be assassin.

"Baldur's Balls! I've never heard of such a Talent."

"Neither have I."

"The Jarl will need to be told. The guards, how

were they, when you left them?"

"Still dazed."

"And the prisoners? They're unharmed?"

"Yes sir. I arrived just in time."

"Good. I would not have enjoyed telling the Jarl that we let two women be killed while in our custody, even if they are accused of murder."

A masterful understatement, if I've ever heard one.

"We need to secure them. That sneak could return at any time to finish what you interrupted. You shouldn't have left them unguarded, even to bring me this information." Hahlf turned to the armsman. "Rouse the next watch and summon a Healer to the gaol."

The man sprinted away.

"Actually, sir, I moved the prisoners to a secure location before coming to you. They're safe."

"Excellent. Where are they? Now that we know there's a threat, we'll move them back to their cells and increase the guard."

Now for the fun part. "No sir. The prisoners will be safer if few know where they are. Someone wants them dead, and that person has a Talent at his command that can put two healthy men into a passive daze for at least several minutes. We don't know how many that Talent can affect at once, if he can use that Talent at a distance, or only by touch. I don't want to find out through failure what other resources that person has."

Hahlf's brows drew down in a frown. "Your caution does you credit Aren, but it's misplaced. *I* am responsible for them. Tell me where they are."

"No, Commander. My caution is *not* misplaced. My orders from Lord Fendrikanin and the Jarl were to bring those women to Quartzholm and keep them safe. So far, I've only met part of that of that duty. I mean to fulfill the rest as well."

"You don't think my guards are competent to protect them?" Hahlf asked in a dangerous tone.

"I'm not suggesting you'd do less than your utmost to protect the prisoners," Aren said. "But I must fulfill my duty in the way I deem best. The women are safer where they are than they would be in the gaol, and in no danger of escaping. More guards will only draw attention to them and show the assassin where to attack. I believe secrecy is the better protection."

"I should have you flogged." Commander Hahlf's mouth tightened.

Aren wondered if the man was considering how many lashes to order.

Then Hahlf growled, "Very well. But when the Jarl summons them they had better appear, or you'll be taking their place in a cell."

"Thank you, sir." Aren turned to go, pausing at the door. "I'd like the honor of Tracking the assassin. I believe I'd have an advantage since I fought with him."

"Granted. But be careful, and take another man with you. A wounded beast is more dangerous when it's cornered."

Aren nodded and said, "Well I know it." Then he added, "Perhaps you should put an additional guard on Lord Vali until we have this Loki-spawn in custody."

"Are you teaching me my duties, now?" Hahlf snarled. "I already thought of that. Now get out."

Aren made his way back to the gaol to pick up the assassin's spoor. The Healer was leaving and the guards now seemed alert and hale. He pointed at the one that hadn't leered at Benoia. "What's your Talent?"

The tall young man lowered his blond brows in a perplexed frown. "I'm a Cat's Eye."

"Good. Do you want to catch the man who nearly made you fail in your duty?"

"Yes!"

"Then come with me."

The guard nodded and followed Aren from the gaol.

"Hey! You can't just walk away from your post!" the other guard protested.

"He can, by order of Commander Hahlf," Aren shot back. "Besides, you don't have much to guard at the moment, now do you?"

Aren stopped briefly at the armory to borrow a bow and quiver full of arrows since he didn't want to take the time to go home for his own. The young guard chose his knife and a throwing stick.

"What's your name, Cat's Eye?"

"Pavel."

"What do you remember of what happened?"

"Not much. A man came to the gaol and held out his hand in greeting. After that, it was like I was sleeping, until the Healer woke me."

Thank the gods. Pavel and his fellow guard wouldn't be able to tell anyone that it was Aren who had taken their prisoners.

"Do you think the women, I mean, the prisoners are all right?"

Pavel went up a notch in Aren's estimation. "Yes. They were taken to a safe place."

"Thank Baldur!" The relief in the young guard's face seemed genuine. "And thank you, sir, for giving me this chance to redeem myself. What do you want me to do?"

Aren nodded. "Your job is to watch my back while I Track this Loki's spawn. I'll be intent on his path, so I'll need your eyes on everything else."

Pavel nodded. "Yes, sir."

Aren gave Pavel a sharp glance at the courtesy, but it was clear the man had spoken sincerely, not mockingly. He didn't know Aren's past. As far as the young guard was concerned, Aren was just the man who was keeping him from complete disgrace.

Aren tracked his quarry as easily as he would a wounded buck. He didn't need his Talent to follow the trail of blood spatters through the corridors. Aren enjoyed a grim satisfaction in knowing he'd left his mark on the spawn who'd meant to murder Annikke and Benoia in their beds. Although the killer must know he'd be pursued, the man attempted no subterfuge or misdirection. Instead, he'd headed straight for a storage closet on the next floor up. Ripped linen indicated he'd bound his wound, and when his track continued, the blood trail was absent.

The lack of visible sign mattered not at all to Aren. Even though the assassin now began taking an erratic path to throw off pursuit, his route was as clear to Aren as if the man had left chalk marks on the floor pointing the way.

Eventually, the man slipped out of the castle by the door to the kitchen garden. The guard there was dazed, just as those in the gaol had been. Aren slapped the man awake, and then continued onward through the garden gate, the shadows behind the stables, and past the barracks. When he reached the door beside the postern gate, Aren estimated he was less than a candlemark behind, and catching up. His quarry might be bleeding less, but the man had lost a fair amount of blood before binding his wound. He wasn't moving at his best speed.

Aren and Pavel spent more time than Aren wanted awakening the gate guards from their Talent induced oblivion, but honor wouldn't let him leave the gate unguarded. Even more time was wasted explaining to the embarrassed and confused men why the small gate was unlocked and Aren and his companion were slapping them. Aren was on the verge of regretting his honorbound choice, when comprehension filtered into the guards' addled minds, and they waved him on his way.

Arrow nocked and ready, Aren trailed the assassin through the dark streets of the village past quiet shops and taverns. Dawn was still over a candlemark away, but the moon's silvery glow cast enough light to cut sharp shadows across the alleyways. The fellow was growing more clever now, doubling back and crossing his own trail. His tactics slowed Aren's pursuit, but didn't make his task impossible.

Not long before dawn, Aren followed the track as it slipped out of the village via a drainage alley, and headed across open country straight toward the forest. Aren grinned as he jogged after his quarry. "Now we've got him," he murmured. The fool was heading for the environment that Aren felt most comfortable in, far more so than the village streets.

"Won't it be easier for him to hide in the forest?" Pavel asked.

"Not from me. Or you, for that matter."

The eastern sky was just beginning to grey as Aren stepped into the shadows under the trees. The forest's cool breath welcomed him but he moved cautiously. Behind him, Pavel's movements were less than silent. Aren glanced back as a twig snapped with a small crack that sounded loud in the quiet.

"Sorry. I'm not much of a woodsman."

Aren shrugged. "Just be careful." There wasn't time to teach him now. At least with his Cat's Eye Talent, Pavel wouldn't trip over unseen rocks and roots.

In the distance, the woodland's inhabitants began to awaken, with a chirp here, a rustle there, but around Aren, the branches and bracken were still. At least Pavel had stopped shuffling along behind him.

Aren stopped. Listened. Felt for the trail with his Talent. And realized that his prey was as skilled in woodcraft as he was.

Instinct made Aren turn and raise his bow. Ten paces back, Pavel stood still, his eyes glazed and unseeing. Much closer, the assassin rushed toward Aren, bare hand outstretched, the other wielding a long blade.

Annikke, Benoia, and Vali broke their fast with a meal of nuts and fruit, cold meat, warm bread, and soft cheese. Simple fare, but delicious and plentiful, thanks to the excess provided because Vali was in Emergence. Or maybe the kitchen had been told he had "guests."

The dining room where they ate was as big as the main room of her cottage, and the table they sat at was circled by an inlaid pattern of multi-colored wood that depicted hunters and the stags and boars they pursued. Annikke hadn't fully comprehended Vali's rank while they were on the trail, when he'd been dressed in plain garb and just as grubby as she and Benoia had been. Clearly the Jarl held Lady Solveig in high regard, to assign her heir a suite furnished with such beautiful things and with more rooms than he could use.

Annikke and Benoia had slept well on a wool-stuffed mattress under a quilted comforter. Vali had offered them each their own bed, but with a glance at her foster-daughter, Annikke had known they'd both sleep better comforted by the other's presence.

They'd just finished eating when Norva returned from her errand, bringing clothing to replace the robes they'd been given the night before. The blue dress Benoia donned complimented the girl's fair hair and made her big blue eyes luminous, but was slightly too large for her. It made her look as if she was only twelve. Annikke's forest green gown, however, fit perfectly.

Within moments of putting on their new clothing a

young runner arrived, summoning Vali and his guests to appear before the Jarl. Vali's brows rose at the carefully worded invitation and dismissed the runner. "It's time, ladies."

"I wish Aren were here," Annikke said, covering her bright hair with a scarf. Her feelings made no sense. She barely knew the man, but there was something about him that made her feel safe.

Vali regarded her as if he understood what she hadn't said. "Perhaps he'll meet us there. In the meantime, I'll do my best in his absence."

Annikke felt her face grow warm. "I didn't mean—"

"I know," Vali interrupted. "No offense was taken."

Annikke tried to swallow her fear. At least they'd be going to their doom clean and well-dressed.

chapter twenty-two

OUTSIDE OF VALI'S SUITE, two additional guards stood watch, supplementing the one that had been on duty by the stair the night before.

"We're to accompany you, my lord."

Annikke's heart sped up, if that was possible, but Vali appeared merely curious. "Why the armed escort? Is there some threat to the peace?"

The guards exchanged a look. "Someone attacked the guards in the gaol last night, my lord, and helped the prisoners to escape."

Benoia made a small sound of distress.

"No need to worry, miss," the other guard said. "The prisoners will soon be caught. One of our best Tracker Talents is on their trail."

"That's good to know" Vali exchanged a concerned look with Annikke and patted her hand where it rested on his arm. "In the meantime. I'm glad you're here to help keep these ladies safe."

The guard nodded and led them down the hall to

the stairway, the other armsman following. The same passages that had been deserted the night before now bustled with activity. Servants stood aside and as they passed, and the lords and ladies they saw nodded courteously, even if most of them gave her hair a startled second glance. Annikke almost wanted to laugh. What a difference a bath, good clothing, and a noble escort made. If all those people knew she and Benoia were the escaped prisoners, accused of murder, they'd treat the two of them very differently.

Now that she was rested, Annikke could pay attention to her surroundings, and she had to keep herself from gawking at the beauty. Heavy wood doors were exquisitely carved, each with a unique image. Statues of the gods and their mounts stood for newel posts at the top and bottom of each staircase. Light reflected in from cleverly placed openings, even well away from outside walls, bringing the rose quartz to life.

After traversing several hallways and multiple flights of stairs, the guard stopped outside a set of open double doors bracketed by two more guards. Vali quietly identified himself and one of them stepped into the opening and announced, "Lord Vali, and Mistresses Annikke and Benoia, my lord."

A man of perhaps forty summers sat on the ornately carved chair on the low dais at the other end of the room. His auburn hair was highlighted with sun-bleached strands and he wore his beard short. Broad shoulders filled out a suede tunic dyed the same dark green as her dress. Annikke appreciated Vali's subtle touch. He'd chosen the color of her gown not to match her eyes, but to indicate her loyalty. But where her dress was plain, a hawk embroidered with gold thread swooped across the man's left breast.

The Jarl. Until a week ago, Annikke had never imagined she would see him, and certainly not under these circumstances. A pregnant woman sat beside him, her blond hair braided in a simple style. *Lady Celia.* Her chair was the same size as the Jarl's, indicating her status, but requiring the Lady to rest her feet on a padded stool so her toes didn't dangle like a child's.

Another man, a little younger and clearly related to Lord Dahleven, stood slightly behind the Jarl and to one side. He was dressed in the gray mourning garb of a priest of Baldur. *That must be the Overprest, Father Ragnar, the Jarl's brother.* She'd once heard a skald sing of his exploits in the conflict with the Dark Elves. She'd heard that his Talent was Truth-telling. She hoped that was true—and that the Jarl valued the truth.

Lord Dahleven gestured them forward.

The room was long and narrow, with two long benches close to the dais. Vali escorted Annikke across the smooth rose quartz floor, with Benoia holding her other hand.

Lord Tholvar occupied the bench on the left facing the Jarl. He had two retainers standing behind him, neither of them men Annikke had seen before. As they entered, Tholvar turned to glare at them.

As they advanced, Benoia's stride faltered for a step, possibly because of the look of hatred on Lord Tholvar's face. Annikke was grateful for Vali's confident support, because she wasn't sure if her knees or Benoia's were shaking more. Vali stopped in the wide space between the benches to stand before the Jarl. Vali bowed slightly, and Annikke sank somewhat awkwardly into a low curtsy with Benoia following her example. Curtsying wasn't a skill they'd needed to practice much in their little village.

Lord Dahleven regarded them with an impassive expression. Not a twitch of brow or lips betrayed any shock or fearful curiosity at the sight of her silver hair. His lady, too, had a neutral expression, nor did she guard her belly as if fearful of her Fey influence.

"Rise," Lord Dahleven said. "Mistress Benoia, Lord Tholvar has already told me what happened between you and his son. I'd like to hear your account of the events that bring you here."

Vali whispered, "Courage," in Annikke's ear, patted her hand again, and then went to sit on the right. Norva stood behind the young lord.

"My lord!" Tholvar protested. "What benefit will this provide? You have the facts, while these women will both lie to protect themselves."

Benoia cast a panicked glance at Annikke.

"It's all right, sweetling." Annikke squeezed her foster-daughter's hand. The girl was trembling. "Just tell the truth as best you can."

The Jarl smiled gently. "Good advice, mistress. Now come closer, Benoia, so you don't have to shout."

Annikke gave Benoia's hand another squeeze then released it. She was trembling herself as she moved to stand with Norva behind Vali.

"I was on my way home from treating the wounds of Lord Tholvar's dairyman—he was gored by a bull—when Lord Sveyn accosted me in the forest."

Annikke clenched her hands as Benoia's soft words brought the image of Sveyn atop her foster-daughter to the forefront of her mind. She remembered Benoia's fear and anger and hurt. Remembered her own fury and desire to do violence.

Father Ragnar stepped forward to whisper in his brother's ear just as Lord Tholvar interrupted. "You see, my lord? Lies. Why waste our time on this?"

Lord Dahleven held up his hand palm outward to the lord. "My time, *and yours*, is mine to waste." He turned back to Benoia. "And how was the dairyman when you visited him?"

For a moment Benoia looked confused by the unexpected question, then she said, "He was doing well. The wound was reddened, but the poultice and our, um, other medicines had worked. There was no putrefaction. I left him more herbs to help with the pain, and others for his wife to give him when he talked too soon about returning to work." A little smile played at the corner of her lips. "Men never respect their injuries."

Lady Celia smiled and glanced at the Jarl. "Isn't *that* the truth."

Lord Dahleven shook his head at his wife, but his gaze held affection. "And after you left the dairyman's cottage? You met with Lord Sveyn?"

Benoia swallowed hard and continued her account. Her voice was stronger now than it had been when she started, and Annikke blessed the Jarl for giving Benoia the chance to gather her wits by talking about the thing she knew best—healing.

"Sveyn was waiting in the small clearing near the big oak. I was surprised to see him there, because a storm was coming. He said I was pretty, and that he liked the bold way I flounced about the village." Benoia twisted her fingers together. "I don't *flounce*, my lord. I just go about my business."

Lady Celia was gripping her armrests tightly, her lips pressed together. Annikke thought she looked sympathetic, but it was Lord Dahleven who would pass judgment on Benoia, and his expression was impossible to read.

The Jarl nodded. "Please go on."

Tears flowed down Benoia's cheeks as she continued. Sveyn said he wanted her, and could give her beautiful dresses and jewelry, and invited her up to the manor. She'd said no, and backed away. Sveyn grabbed her, pushed her down and shouted at her to stop being a tease. His grasp had been painful on her arms, on her legs. She'd screamed and pushed at him, but he was too strong. All she'd wanted was for him to *stop*. Suddenly he'd begun screaming, and Annikke had pulled him off of her.

A muscle in Lord Dahleven's jaw jumped as he glanced at Father Ragnar.

"Lies," Lord Tholvar repeated. "She lay in wait for my son, and when he refused to lie with her, she maimed him."

Benoia turned on Lord Tholvar. "That's not what happened!"

"Show us your bruises, then, if you tell the truth."

"She cannot. I healed them. It was all I could do for her." Annikke felt a flutter of panic as she spoke. Had she not done that kindness, Benoia would have evidence to prove what happened. Now they had nothing.

"How convenient," Lord Tholvar said. "And what about the men that she and that Fey-marked witch killed? Can they pay the *weregild* for them?"

Annikke gasped. If the *weregild* fell on her and Benoia, they'd be sold into thralldom to meet it, no matter their blame or innocence.

"Lord Vali, do you have anything to add?" the Jarl asked.

Vali rose. The dirty, Exhausted lad she'd met in the forest was gone. Even her clean and rested friend had been replaced with a young lord whose dignified bearing befit the heir to noble family. "Would those men be the ones that wore no livery or the sigil of any house? I took them to be bandits."

"My lords, if I may?" Norva asked.

Vali nodded, as did Lord Dahleven. Norva came around the bench to stand beside Benoia. "I, and three other women from Forsvaremur, killed men we saw attacking Lord Vali and the two women who had been caring for him. They claimed to be acting on behalf of Lord Tholvar and the Jarl, but I didn't believe them since they were also proposing to rape these women. One of those men escaped, and two days later he attacked again with more men. We prevailed, but only just. The Jarl's actual emissary didn't recognize any of them either."

Annikke noted that Norva didn't mention the intervention of the Elves or Annikke's use of Elven magic to heal Aren.

"Lord Vali, do you agree with this statement?" The Jarl asked.

"I do, my lord."

Annikke could only see a portion of Lord Tholvar's face, but she thought he looked surprised, and then thoughtful.

From behind them, a guard announced, "Lord Sveyn and Lord Fendrikanin."

Annikke's heart took a little leap. Lord Fender hadn't forgotten his pledge to her. Whether he could offer any real help she didn't know, but she would welcome another friend.

Her hope stuttered when she saw his face. His expression wasn't a friendly one. As he came abreast of Benoia he gave her a suspicious glare, and went to stand beside Lady Celia.

Sveyn limped badly, bracing each step with a staff and dragging one foot as he made his way laboriously to the front of the room. Annikke couldn't bring herself to feel any sympathy for the Loki-spawn.

Lord Tholvar jumped up from his bench. "What are you doing here? I told you to stay home. Now everyone can see you!"

"It's not exactly the kind of thing we can keep secret, Father." Sveyn made a face. "And I agreed with Lord Fendrikanin that I should be present to ensure justice prevailed."

"Lord Tholvar, did you send the men who attacked

Annikke and Benoia?" Lord Dahleven asked.

"No, my lord."

"Lord Sveyn, were those men there at your command?"

"Of course not!"

Lord Dahleven nodded. Annikke found herself wondering if they'd been mistaken in placing the blame for the attacks they'd endured at Sveyn's door.

"Then why did they mention you by name?" Benoia demanded.

Her foster-daughter's exclamation startled Annikke, and she blinked in confusion. How could she have doubted that Sveyn was involved?

Lord Dahleven turned to Benoia. "You've had your say," he said firmly, but not unkindly to Benoia. He frowned and glanced at his brother.

Lord Ragnar's forehead was furrowed, as if trying to figure out some puzzle. A moment later his brows lifted as if he was surprised by the solution. He whispered something to the Jarl, who looked startled before his brow clouded with anger.

Annikke twisted her fingers together. An angry lord was a dangerous lord.

But when he spoke to his wife, Lord Dahleven's tone was mild. "My dear, your amulet, if you please?"

Lady Celia's eyes widened, then she lifted a pendant from under her bodice and offered it in her open palm. Her husband clasped her hand over the necklace. Beside Lady Celia, Lord Fender turned a startled expression from his liege to Sveyn, as his expression turned thunderous. The tension in his body suggested he wanted to throttle the young lord. Annikke looked from Father Ragnar, to the Jarl, to Lord Fender. Something had changed, but she didn't know what.

The Jarl narrowed his eyes at Sveyn. "My lord, would you like to reconsider your answer?" His tone held a quiet threat.

Sveyn wobbled on his good leg and staff. "I only told them to take Benoia into custody! If they did more, they overstepped their orders."

That's possible, Annikke thought. The first group of men had only disarmed her. *Maybe the others made a mistake when they tried to kill me and Aren.*

"And what of the assassin that tried to kill them in their cells?" Aren's voice came from the doorway. Every eye turned to watch as he strode forward. Annikke noted that he walked with a slight limp and there was blood on his trews. Had he reopened his wound, or gained a new one? She wanted to make him sit down so she could examine him, but that would have to wait.

Aren stopped within striking distance of Sveyn, but kept his hands fisted at his sides.

"I take it the intruder resisted your invitation to return to Quartzholm?" Lord Dahleven asked.

"Unfortunately, yes," Aren answered in grim tones. "With both Talent and blade."

"Did he speak before he died?"

"Nothing of importance, my lord."

Annikke thought Sveyn released a pent up breath.

"Lord Sveyn," the Jarl asked softly. "What do you know of the man who entered my gaol on a ruse, and left two of my guards dazed and vulnerable to attack?"

"Nothing my lord! How could I? I only just got here with Lord Fendrikanin."

"Oh, please," Lady Celia muttered.

The Jarl's gaze flickered toward his wife with what Annikke thought was a hint of amusement.

"My lord Jarl," Father Ragnar spoke for the first time in a voice like death. "Lord Sveyn has lied thrice to you. Further, he has abused those under his authority. The law is clear."

"No!" Lord Tholvar's face was pale and he sounded

desperate. "I count only two falsehoods! The threshold has not been met."

"Actually, Lord Tholvar, the count is four. He first lied to you," Father Ragnar said, lifting a finger, "when he told you Benoia lay in wait for *him*. He sought to deceive the Jarl regarding the attacks, and their purpose." Two more fingers joined the first. "And he lied again about the assassin." A fourth digit rose.

"He couldn't know about the intruder! He was with Lord Fendrikanin!"

"His commands were already in place, were they not, Lord Sveyn?" Ragni asked with a lifted brow. "If your other men failed to stop Benoia from reaching Quartzholm, your assassin was to prevent her from speaking the truth to Lord Dahleven. Moreover, Lord Sveyn has been attempting to influence us all with his Talent. A form of Persuasion, I believe, that makes everything he says seem true and believable."

Benoia's Talent is to see past illusion to the truth. That's why she wasn't taken in by Sveyn's lies, Annikke thought. "But men of rank are seldom held accountable for taking what they want from a woman," Annikke said. "Why go to so much effort?"

"That witch withered my cock! I'll never enjoy another fuck, never have heirs. And everyone knows about the Jarl's new *laws.* I knew he'd punish me, instead of her. *Me!* I wasn't going to let that bitch get away with it."

"Ah, he speaks the truth at last," Ragni said softly.

"My lord, I ask your mercy," Tholvar said, looking rather sick. "He's my only son!"

"Then you'd better make good alliances for your daughters, with men more honorable than the one you begat," Lady Celia said.

Lord Dahleven shot her a quelling glance. "Lord Sveyn, by your actions you have proven yourself unworthy to care for the land the Elves have shared with us.

You need worry no more about your inability to sire heirs. You are disinherited."

"What? No! Please, my lord, I was angry and afraid and sent those men without thought."

"*Afraid? You* were afraid?" The words leapt out of Annikke before she could stop them. "What of Benoia's fear, when you threw her down on the ground? Or when your men tried to kill her?"

Lord Dahleven raised a hand palm outward to silence her. His lip curled in disgust as he looked again at Sveyn. "Do you believe being driven by fear a defense?"

"My lord, he's young—"

"He is fully twenty summers of age, and long recognized as a man. He will bear the consequences of his actions as a man must."

Father Ragnar whispered something to the Jarl, who raised his sun-lightened brows in apparent surprise. "You're sure?" he asked.

The Overprest nodded.

The Jarl continued in a grim tone. "In addition, you will be stripped of your Talent. You have proven yourself willing to use it to harm others, and I will not leave you able to do so in the future."

Annikke gaped at the harsh sentence. A man without a Talent was regarded as a cripple, even more so than one missing a limb.

"My lord! No! I'm sorry," Sveyn pleaded. "Have mercy I beg of you! I made a mistake."

"You've made more than one, and many more than have ever been discovered, I suspect," Lord Dahleven said. "But I *will* show you mercy—more than you showed the innocent young woman you tried to have killed. You will not be exiled. Instead you'll be restricted to your family's land, living on their sufferance." Lord Dahleven rose. "You are dismissed. Return to your holding."

"But my lord, what life can I live, crippled like this? This deformity is not a proper punishment under your law."

The Jarl paused. Annikke could see his jaw working, as if he was chewing angry words.

Lord Ragnar spoke. "When you hunt a mountain cat, you may get bitten. Bear it."

"No," Benoia said softly. "I'll heal him, if I can."

What? Had she misheard? Annikke turned her disbelieving gaze to her foster-daughter, as did everyone else in the room. "Sweetling?"

"I don't want him telling everyone who will listen about how the servant of the Fey-marked witch destroyed his life." Anger and disgust chased across Benoia's face. "Even without his Talent, some may look at his shriveled leg and believe him, and turn against you. I hate him for what he tried to do to me. To you. If I heal him, his words will just be the bitter ranting of a Talentless man. But I'll need your help."

Annikke drew in a deep breath, then another. The rage in her heart tried to explode. "How can you even *think* of this?" She didn't want to *heal* the Loki-spawn, she wanted to *kill* him for what he tried to do.

Benoia stepped closer to Annikke and took her hands. "I can think of it because I want to go live among the Daughters of Freya in Forsvaremur, and I can't leave you behind to suffer Sveyn's frustration and wrath in my place."

"I could come with you," Annikke said.

Benoia's eyes brightened, but she shook her head. "You have a home among the villagers. Most of them respect you, and many of them even like you. I can't ask you to leave that behind. You've wanted your whole life to be accepted by them."

"You're wise for one so young, mistress Benoia, but I think your fear is greater than the threat. Few will listen to a Talentless man who has been disinherited. Nevertheless, I will give you a choice, Sveyn." Lord Dahleven stepped off the low dais and stopped in front of Tholvar's son. "You may choose whether to be healed and be exiled for two years, or live as you are on your father's lands."

Exile! It wasn't quite a sentence of death, but a man alone in the wildlands, without kin or friends, was vulnerable to injury, starvation, and hungry mountain cats. Permanent deformity or possible death. Annikke thought the choice fitting.

"That's a Loki's bargain!" Tholvar protested.

"Be quiet, Father," Sveyn said.

"Furthermore, whichever you choose, I will have your oath that you will visit no harm on Annikke or Benoia, nor on anyone under your authority ever again. Not a wife, a child, nor the boy who cleans your latrines. Will you so swear?"

"My lord! You cannot mean to sanction dark *seidhr* by letting these ... witches perform yet more of their magic on my son?" Lord Tholvar objected.

"My leg and my cock are as shriveled as a dried plum, Father. What worse harm could they do?" Sveyn turned back to Lord Dahleven. "If she can heal me, I'll swear anything you like."

"You misunderstand. She won't even *attempt* to heal you until you give your oath."

"And when I give my oath, she'll have no reason to heal me."

"Would you prefer exile as you are?"

Sveyn bowed his head. "No, my lord." With great difficulty he knelt on his one good knee and set his staff aside.

The Jarl drew his sword and presented it hilt first to Sveyn. "Give me your oath."

"May Baldur witness my vow," Sveyn began as he

touched the grip, then swore what the Jarl had demanded. He finished by reciting the traditional words, "If I fail in my honor, may every man's hand turn against me and this sword pierce my disloyal heart, and may all know me as Oathbreaker."

The weight of Sveyn's oath resonated in Aren's soul. No man could witness such a vow and not feel it. No man could speak those words and take them lightly. His father had spoken those words. And he had paid the price of breaking that oath.

A price his father had willingly paid. Aren finally understood that the cost to his father of keeping his honor, of leaving the woman he loved when she needed him, would have been too high. His father's pride and stubbornness had kept him from being able to see his alternatives, but it had been his love for Aren's mother that had forced his hand. He'd chosen love over honor.

For the first time in his life, Aren understood his father's decision, and his mother's loyalty to his father's memory.

"Sveyn, you may return with Lord Tholvar to his rooms and await Annikke and Benoia there," the Jarl said, sheathing his sword. "If their healing is successful, you will be given a bow, a quiver of twenty arrows, and a dagger, and escorted to the borders of this province. You may return two summers from now."

Sveyn nodded, then struggled to stand. His damaged leg was too weak. "I need help," he said after a moment. With a nod from Tholvar, his two retainers stepped to either side of Sveyn and lifted him with a hand under each arm. They stayed beside him as he hobbled out of the audience chamber.

Tholvar lingered long enough to say, "I swore fealty to you, my lord, and this is how you honor it? You've thrown away any support I might have given your new law. You can play havoc with tradition without my help."

"Are you sure, Lord Tholvar?" Lady Celia said. "Without a male heir, the new law would allow your eldest daughter to inherit, rather than your cousin. Your lands would remain with your line."

Aren noted that Lord Dahleven didn't censure his wife for her comment, just lifted a brow and smiled slightly. Lord Tholvar glared for a moment, and then made a non-committal grunt before making a minimal nod of courtesy and stalking out.

When he was gone, Lord Dahleven said, "I'm sorry, Celia. Without his support, the other lords aren't likely to approve the law at the Althing this summer. Maybe next year."

The lady didn't appear distressed. "We'll see. It'll depend on which is greater, Tholvar's self-interest or his stubborn anger."

"My lord," Vali said. "I have a boon to ask of you."

"Yes?"

"Forsvaremur needs a good Tracker Talent, and always welcomes men of honor. Aren came to my aid not knowing my rank or family. I'd take it as a personal favor if you'd release him from his oath of service to you, and let him come into mine."

The breath stopped in Aren's throat. Swearing fealty to a man of Lord Vali's rank would go far in cleansing his family name.

"Are you sure you want such an insubordinate man in your service?" the Jarl asked. "He clearly has a tendency to solve problems without consulting those in command. Did you know, he made off with my prisoners and stashed them away for their protection without even a by-your-leave?"

It had been too much to hope that Commander Hahlf would keep Aren's defiance to himself. Aren steeled himself, ready to accept whatever punishment the Jarl chose. He stood by his choice to hide the women with Vali.

Vali grinned. "I'm well aware of his tendency for independent thought. It makes him more desirable to my thinking, rather than less."

"Indeed. As it happens, Aren's oath of service is to Lord Fendrikanin, not to me—yet. Aren, you have a choice before you, will you swear fealty to me, or to Lord Vali?"

chapter twenty-three

ANNIKKE HELD HER BREATH. This was what Aren had been hoping for. A new beginning. A chance to return honor to his name. And now not only the heir to a neighboring Jarldom but the Jarl of Quartzholm wanted him. She hadn't thought there could be room in her heart for anything more than the relief she'd felt for Benoia, and the grief of her leaving, but now joy crowded in. Aren deserved this. So why did he look as though he might lose his breakfast?

"My lord," Aren said to Vali, "I'm honored by your request, more than you know, but before you offer to take me into your household there's something you should know—"

"I know more than you think. Lady Solveig and her husband taught me a thing or two while waiting for my Talent to Emerge. I would not seek the oath of a man I did not understand—and trust."

Annikke bounced on her toes, unable to contain her happiness for Aren.

Aren nodded, unspeaking. He looked into Annikke's eyes.

Everyone in the room followed suit. Suddenly Annikke no longer felt like bouncing. For a moment she
wanted to escape the weight of their attention, but then,
as it had in the forest, Aren's calm brown gaze steadied
and centered her.

"If I swear to Lord Vali, my home will be closer to
Benoia," he said.

"But Quartzholm welcomes the Elves and their
friends," Lord Dahleven said. "And good Healers are always needed."

Aren continued as if the Jarl hadn't spoken. "We
haven't known each other for very long, but I think we
understand each other better than many do at the out-
set." Aren stepped closer. "You have courage and
strength and compassion, and the most beautiful hair
I've ever seen."

Annikke's heart pounded and her stomach buzzed
like a charm of hummingbirds had taken up residence. *What is he saying?*

She recognized the look that filled Aren's eyes.
Guarded hope. The same feeling that filled her so unexpectedly.

But hope was dangerous. Too often it lifted you up
only to trip you at the next turn. Annikke sought Benoia's reaction, and found her foster-daughter grinning
with excited anticipation. She had as much reason as
Annikke to fear hope, but she didn't. Instead she was
ready to leap into change. To go where she'd never been
before.

It was easier to answer Benoia's hope. "Of course I
release you from your service, you goose. In my heart,
you haven't been a servant to me since that first Midsummer's night. Be happy."

Benoia hugged her, and Annikke held the girl

tightly, wishing she didn't have to let her go. When they stepped back from each other, Annikke found herself confronted with Aren's hopeful gaze again.

"I would like my wife to be happy in the place I serve. Where do you think that would be?"

Wife?

The question must have shown in her expression, because he added, "If you will have me."

"What about your mother and daughter?" Annikke whispered.

The corner of Aren's mouth curved up in a wry smile. "Tandra's a romantic. She urged me to save you. And Mother will come to love you. As I have."

In her belly the hummingbirds zoomed and trilled. She was being asked to dance steps she didn't know. No one had asked her to dance at all, ere now. But like Benoia, she found she was ready to learn.

"I'd like to live in Forsvaremur."

"With me?" Aren asked.

"With you," Annikke promised.

epilogue

One year later,
Midsummer's Eve

"I think your Talent with plants exceeds mine," Annikke said, as Tandra closed the wound from a broken branch on the apple tree behind their cottage.

Tandra grinned. "Don't let the Elves find out."

Annikke smiled, not minding the teasing. They both knew the Elves wouldn't take Tandra the way they had Annikke. Gaelon and his brother had visited Annikke and Aren several times in their new home in Forsvaremur, and Annikke had welcomed them. At first, she'd accepted them because they'd helped save Aren's life, but later because they'd become friends. Their glamor made them appear to be no more than merchants to the neighbors.

"Let me help you," Tandra said, as Annikke struggled to her feet.

Annikke let the girl help her stand. She was near term, and getting up from the ground was growing more difficult by the day.

"I wish Benoia was here, already," Tandra said. "You've taught me a lot, but—"

"Don't worry, she'll be here in less than a fortnight." Annikke smiled. "She wouldn't miss the birth of her sister."

Annikke and Aren had moved their family to a cottage with a little land on the outskirts of the village surrounding Forsvaremur. Annikke had declined Vali's invitation to live inside his castle; she and Tandra needed to have plants nearby to use their Talents on. A few months after settling in, Torlon had taken one look at her and confirmed her suspicion that she was expecting.

"*Another* girl?" Aren had said, pretending to be disappointed that she wasn't carrying a son, but Annikke had seen the happiness shining in his eyes. "I guess we'll just have to keep trying."

"Supper's ready," Morla called them in for the midday meal.

Aren's mother had been taken aback at having a new daughter by marriage thrust into her life so abruptly. She'd been put out by having Annikke take her place as the woman of the house, until she found out that Annikke had healing skills. When she hadn't just soothed Morla's pain but eliminated it entirely, Morla had welcomed her new daughter by marriage with open arms.

Aren met them at the door and the sight of him made Annikke smile, as it always did. His brown eyes never failed to warm her all the way through, and today they were dancing with excitement.

"What is it?" she asked.

Instead of answering, he kissed her, and then stepped aside. "Surprise!"

Benoia stood behind him, beaming. She was brown

from the sun, and new muscles defined her upper arms. Living among the Daughters of Freya clearly agreed with her.

Annikke opened her arms and hugged her foster-daughter, who had to lean over the babe in her belly. "You came early!"

"Well, sometimes babies do too, so I thought I'd snatch a little of your attention for myself before my new sister hogs it all."

Benoia answered with a smile, but Annikke could see concern in her eyes. "Babies get born every day, sweetling, and I have two of the best midwives a woman could ask for. I'm not worried."

Benoia nodded. "Is that Morla's famous baked squash I smell?"

"It is," Morla said with exaggerated pride. "And bread pudding to follow."

"Then let's get to it!" Aren eagerly rubbed his hands together.

By the time desert had been eaten and the dishes washed, Annikke was sure that Benoia had arrived just in time. Her foster-daughter had just snapped Tandra on the rear with the drying towel when a particularly strong contraction made her gasp.

"Are you all right?" Aren asked, ever attentive.

"I think this girl is in a hurry to meet her sisters," Annikke said.

Benoia nodded. "Gaelon said she was going to come early."

"Really? Why didn't he tell *me*?" Annikke said.

"He didn't want you to fret."

"I don't fret," Annikke complained.

Benoia exchanged a look with Tandra. "Of course not. Now just relax. We'll take care of everything." Benoia's words were calm enough, but her eyes were alight with excitement.

Annikke laughed. "Well, I think I'll have *something* to contribute."

Several hours later, Katrinja made her debut in the usual way. After tidying up, Annikke leaned back in Aren's arms with their new daughter at her breast. Morla rested in a nearby rocking chair while Tandra and Benoia sat at the foot of the bed, leaning against the posts, looking very pleased with themselves.

They deserved to feel smug. They'd remembered everything she'd taught them and had kept calm throughout. Feeling tired and happy, Annikke teased, "See, I told you there was nothing to worry about."

Benoia and Tandra exchanged a look. "Yes, mother," they said in unison.

A knock on the door made Annikke stiffen and hold her breath. Aren's arms tightened around her, but a moment later she blew out her fear with a shaky laugh. "Sorry. Old memories."

Tandra went to open the door, and returned a moment later. "Old friends," she said, standing aside to let Gaelon crowd into the bedroom with Torlon and Vali.

"News travels fast," Aren said. "Katrinja hasn't been here much more than a candlemark."

"How did you know?" Tandra asked.

Vali shrugged. "I'm here because these two came to get me."

Tandra turned to the Elves, who at the moment wore their merchant glamour.

Gaelon answered, looking embarrassed. "We didn't, not precisely. I wagered you'd still be in labor, but Torlon said your daughter would already be a day old."

"You bet on the birth of my baby?" Annikke would have been outraged, except that it was so predictable.

"At least I won," Gaelon said.

Vali leaned close to kiss Annikke's cheek, diverting

her attention. "Congratulations on your newest beautiful daughter." He ran a single finger over Katrinja's brown fuzz. "So soft! But I expect she'll wish she had her mother's silver locks when she grows up. She'll have to make do with a silver rattle instead," which he handed to Aren.

"And for the mother, I brought this." Vali laid a hair clasp with the image of the Forsvaremur stag crafted with sparkling black stones in her hand. "It will be stunning in your hair."

Annikke stared, shocked by the wealth Lord Vali had just given her. "It's beautiful! But it's too much."

Vali smiled gently. "My mother had it made for you, so it must be exactly right for the woman who helped save my life. And I don't want you to hide it away in a box. I want you to *wear* it."

"I will." Annikke pulled Vali down so she could kiss his cheek, provoking a blush.

"We have a gift as well," Gaelon said, producing a spray of delicate white blooms which he touched to Katrinja's head. "I name you Ellian, Elf-friend. May you sing like the lark, dance with the lightness of leaves upon the wind, and if ever you have need, call our names thrice, and we will answer."

Aren held out his hand and clasped Torlon's wrist. "Thank you. No man could have better friends."

"I should say not," Vali said, and everyone laughed.

"And now, because we *are* good friends, we'll depart, so mother and child can get some well-earned rest," Gaelon said. "Besides, it's still Midsummer's eve, and we have debts to settle."

~ ~ ~

thank you!

Thanks for reading *DEBTS* and letting me entertain you for a few hours. If you enjoyed this book, please tell your friends and take a few minutes to leave a review on the site where you purchased it. It doesn't have to be long and involved, just a few thoughts about what you liked will help other readers know why they might enjoy it, too. Not many readers leave reviews, but authors depend on word of mouth and reviews from their fans. Your opinion matters!

Please follow me on Amazon and BookBub and make sure you sign up for your free stories, too! My newsletter subscribers will be the first to find out about new releases, sales, and special offers. I won't flood your inbox, and I won't share your email, ever.

ABOUT the AUTHOR

Frankie Robertson writes fantasy and romantic fiction with an otherworldly twist. She also writes the sensual *Victorian Secret Romance* series inspired by mythology, fairy-tales, and cryptozoology as Francesca Rose.

Frankie has lived all over the country, but now lives in the Sonoran desert with her husband in southern Arizona. Her backyard is often visited by hawks, coyotes, javelinas, and bobcats, which don't get along well with the bunnies, quail, and lizards. She brings a varied background to her writing, including experience as an investigator with the Western Society for Paranormal Research.

BOOKS BY FRANKIE ROBERTSON:

The Vinlanders' Saga
DANGEROUS TALENTS
FORBIDDEN TALENTS
DEBTS
DARK WINTER'S NIGHT

The Celestial Affairs Series
LIGHTBRINGER
GUARDIAN
APOSTATE

Celestial Affairs: The Trust
BETRAYED BY TRUST

Stand-alone Titles
VEILED MIRROR
NIGHT MOVES: A Short Story Sampler

TITLES WRITTEN AS FRANCESCA ROSE:

The Victorian Secret Romance Series
WITH HEART TO HEAR
YETI IN THE MIST
YETI YULETIDE

www.ingramcontent.com/pod-product-compliance
Lightning Source LLC
Chambersburg PA
CBHW020618180626
46810CB00007B/2839